MONSTER
OF THE
MONTH CLUB

DIAN CURTIS REGAN

MONSTER
OF THE
MONTH
CLUB

Illustrated by Laura Cornell

HENRY HOLT AND COMPANY | NEW YORK

For
Lee Wardlaw
(the November selection)
with much admiration

Henry Holt and Company, Inc.
Publishers since 1866
115 West 18th Street
New York, New York 10011

Henry Holt is a registered trademark of Henry Holt and Company, Inc.

Published in Canada by Fitzhenry & Whiteside Ltd.,
195 Allstate Parkway, Markham, Ontario L3R 4T8.

Library of Congress Cataloging-in-Publication Data
Regan, Dian Curtis.
Monster of the Month Club / Dian Curtis Regan; illustrated by Laura Cornell.
p. cm.
Summary: Twelve-year-old Rilla's life becomes chaotic when
someone anonymously enrolls her in the Monster of the Month Club
and little living monsters start to arrive in the mail.
[1. Monsters—Fiction.] I. Cornell, Laura, ill. II. Title.
PZ7.R25854Mo 1994 [Fic]—dc20 94-3405

ISBN 0-8050-3443-9
First Edition—1994
Printed in the United States of America on acid-free paper. ∞

1 3 5 7 9 10 8 6 4 2

Contents

1

What the Mail Brought

Rilla didn't believe it until the first one arrived. She'd passed it off as someone's idea of a dumb joke.

But then it came.

It came in a cardboard box the same size as one of her aunt Poppy's shoe boxes. (Aunt Poppy's feet were enormous.)

Rilla had walked down Hollyhock Road to collect mail—one of her morning chores at the bed and breakfast run by her mother and aunt.

As she piled mail into a cloth bag, a mysterious noise made her stop chomping her Grape-a-Lot gum and listen.

Scritch-scritch-scritch.

Curiosity made her brush snow off the curb for a dry spot to sit and investigate. Was the mail making noises?

Steadying the bag between her ankles, she shuffled bills, advertisements, and requests for information about the B & B.

The box!

Shoving everything else aside, Rilla yanked the box from the bag and gave it a brisk shake, holding it to one ear.

SCRITCH-SCRITCH-SCRITCH!

The noise was louder, angrier. And unless her imagination was teasing her, she heard a tiny, tiny yelp.

Quickly she scanned the mailing label. The box wasn't addressed to the bed and breakfast. It was addressed to her!

The return label read:

M.O.T.M. Club
Gaborone, Botswana

Rilla shivered in the January chill as she stared at the initials. Where had she seen them before?

Stuffing everything into the cloth bag, she jumped to her feet, dashed down Hollyhock Road, and slipped through a gap in the tall privacy pines circling the generous front yard of the Victorian house.

She raced across snow-streaked grass, up the wide steps of the veranda, and under a sign that read:

HARMONY HOUSE BED AND BREAKFAST
PEACE TO EVERY ONE

Rilla shouldered through the double oak doors, dumped the mail on an antique sideboard, then shoved the box under her jacket in case she ran into anyone who might ask the wrong question. Like "What is *that*?"

Bounding up the curved stairway to the green floor (green carpet, green herbs decorating the wallpaper), she race-walked down the hallway. (No running past occupied rooms or it might disturb guests.)

Under her jacket, the box began to wiggle—like the kittens in the barn did whenever she tried to smuggle one to her room.

Worried, Rilla thrust the box forward, holding it at arm's length. What was inside? Should she be afraid? The thumpety-thumping of her heart told her she already was.

She dashed up the second stairway to the blue floor (blue carpet, blue moons and stars on the walls). Lucky she hadn't run into any—

"Hey!" came a voice from behind as she passed suite B-2.

Rilla whirled. José, the musician from Montana, stepped from his room. He'd stayed a few extra days after playing at a New Year's Eve bash. His hair, still wet from the shower, was as long as Aunt Poppy's.

"Hey," she said back to him.

He pointed to the box in her outstretched arms. "Is that for me?"

"No!" Rilla bent her elbows so it didn't look as though whatever she carried was about to explode.

He stepped closer, peering at the label. "What is it?"

Uh-oh, the dreaded question. "It's . . . um . . . something somebody sent me." *Well, it's true,* she added to herself.

José cocked his head to listen. "Whatever it is, it's alive." He whispered the words as if the obvious was news to Rilla. Grinning, he added, "When I was your age, I smuggled all kinds of creatures to my room. Of course, my mother always found out, then—" He made a slicing motion across his neck with one finger.

Rilla returned his grin with a feeble one. Her heart had flip-flopped when he'd said the word "creatures."

"Rill!" came her mother's voice from two floors below. "Did you forget it's a school day?"

"Coming!" Rilla backed down the hallway.

"Hey," said José. The hall light glinted off the diamond in his ear. "I hope I get to see *it* later." He winked on the word "it."

Rilla was tempted to say, "No way, José." But that would have been rude.

Clutching the box, she hurried up the creaky wooden steps at the end of the blue hallway. Her room was actually the attic, since all the bedrooms were reserved for guests who came to stay a night, a weekend—or more, like Mr. Tamerow with the Australian accent, who traveled the globe on business. (He liked to say *globe* instead of *world*.)

At the top of the steps, Rilla unlocked the door with the key dangling on a silver chain around her neck. (All the other bedroom doors locked, so why not hers?)

The attic was nearly as large as her classroom at Pickering Elementary, where she went before Mom started home-schooling her.

It was bright, too, with windows on three sides so she could look any direction she pleased (almost). This morning, the north windows shimmered with a thin glaze of ice.

"Finally," she said, trying to assure whatever was now causing the box to wobble *big* time that she *did* plan to free it. She hoped it was the right thing to do.

Rilla placed the package gently on the honeycomb-patterned quilt covering her water bed. But before releasing the box's occupant, there was something she needed to check.

Yanking open the bottom drawer of her dresser, she drew out the ancient cookie tin that held treasures she liked to keep:

- a perfect four-leaf clover saved from the blades of Aunt Poppy's Backyard Ride-a-Mower

- a pencil borrowed from Joshua Banks (her one true love) and never returned because he'd touched it

- letters from Mr. Tamerow with postmarks from around the *globe*

- the complete lyrics to her favorite song, "I'll Love You Till My Pickup's Lost Its Shine"

And the card.

There it was.

Rilla had received it the day after Christmas. She'd thought it was a Christmas card from Joshua Banks, mailed late after she mailed him three. (Two anonymously because they were mushy, and one with her proper name on it because it was religious.)

But it wasn't a Christmas card from Joshua Banks.

She turned the crumpled envelope over and studied the matching initials: M.O.T.M. Club. But the card was not from Botswana. Its return address read Oklahoma City.

Rilla had wracked her brain trying to figure out who might send her a gift from Oklahoma. José was from

Montana, but he traveled a lot to *gigs,* as he called them.

Aunt Poppy was always ordering stuff from catalogs, so it could have been her. Could have been Mr. Tamerow, too, and even Joshua Banks had gone to Oklahoma once to visit his grandparents.

The possibility of Joshua Banks's sending the gift made her heart skyrocket. "I can hope, can't I?" she mumbled.

Then there was her father. The thought of *him* made her hands tremble as she drew out the mysterious card—the one she'd studied a zillion times since Christmas. Her father could be *anywhere.* Oklahoma or the moon, for all she knew.

Blanking thoughts of her father from her mind, she focused on the candy-cane-striped card printed in bright red letters:

> *Happy Holidays*
> To: Rilla Harmony Earth
> From: ?
> Congratulations!
> You have received
> a gift membership
> to the
> *Monster of the Month Club*

SCRITCH-SCRITCH-SCRITCH!

Now the box was shaking as if a nest of wild hornets, boiling in anger, was trapped inside.

Rilla scrambled off the bed.

The sides of the box began to bulge.

She covered her eyes with both hands, peeking between her fingers to watch.

The mailing tape ripped and split.

Then, with a dull pop, the end of the box broke free.

2

Icicle's Popsicles

Rilla backed clear to the far south window as she watched the package unwrap itself—her gaze locked on the opened end of the box.

Seconds later a furry *thing* crawled out on its hands and haunches.

It stood, gulping for air until it seemed to get its fill.

Rilla inched closer for a better look.

The monster's fur was silver, spiking straight to the sky like Tina Welter's hair. Its tail bushed out full and fluffy like a squirrel's. And its face . . . well, its face was the ugliest one Rilla had ever seen.

She tried not to stare, but she wanted to count its eyes. Six, no *seven*. Seven eyes. No ears (that she could see), a pointy nose, and tiny fangs peeking from each side of its jaw.

It glared at her with all seven eyes, kicked the box out of the way with one furry paw, then high-stepped on its hind legs across the bouncy water bed as best it could.

Plowing its way into the ensemble of stuffed animals covering Rilla's pillow, it flung a rhino one way, a walrus the other, then snuggled down in the empty spot, curling into a ball with its head on a fat penguin's stomach.

Before Rilla could edge nearer, it was snoring little monster snores.

Gingerly she picked up the box. A piece of paper fluttered onto the quilt. It read:

Monster of the Month Club

January Selection

Name: Icicle   *Gender:* Male

Homeland: Botswana

Likes: Popsicles, frozen yogurt, iced lemonade

Keep in a cool, dry place.

"This can't be happening," Rilla whispered. He— Icicle—was a real, live monster. What was she supposed to do with him?

"Rilla Harmony Earth!"

Rilla raced to the door, opening it a crack.

Aunt Poppy, vacuum in one hand, duster in the other, peered up the narrow attic stairs. Her waist-length hair was tied in a ponytail, covered with a bandanna. She wore her typical housecleaning clothes: faded blue jeans and a worn T-shirt that read: REPENT AND RECYCLE.

"What are you doing up there? Your mom is ready to start your lessons."

"Straightening up," Rilla said, knowing an answer like that would be rock-and-roll music to her aunt's cleaning-binge ears. "Be right down."

Rilla closed the door and locked it. Just to be safe. Even though she needn't worry about Aunt Poppy coming up the stairs.

That's what Rilla liked best about her attic room. No one came up here. With a dozen bedrooms to clean, her mom and aunt refused to clean one more when she was "perfectly capable of cleaning it her-self."

Rilla had been taking care of the attic and its tiny bathroom since she was old enough to change sheets, dump laundry down a chute to the basement, and run a duster around the floor every week or three.

Tiptoeing back to the bed, she knelt, moving her face close to study the B & B's newest guest—one who had *not* checked in at the registration desk. He smelled faintly of corrugated cardboard.

Icicle opened four of his eyes, narrowing them at her.

"Hello-o-o, little monster," she singsonged, the way her mother talked to the kittens. "Can you speak?"

His insulted look told her he didn't appreciate the baby talk. Stretching onto his back, he crossed his fuzzy ankles, then rubbed his stomach. Did that mean he was hungry?

Rilla touched the side of his head—looking for ears. Yes, he had ears—small and egg-shaped, hidden by raggedy fur.

He cringed, batting her hand away.

"Okay, Icicle," she began, dropping the baby talk. "I'm Rilla. I guess I'm your owner now."

He snickered, as if the opposite was true. At least he seemed to understand her. Was English spoken in Botswana?

"Are you hungry?"

He patted his stomach again with a look that said, *Do I have to repeat myself?*

"Okay, here's the deal." Pausing, Rilla smoothed the imprint of monster claw steps from her quilt, then rescued the rhino and walrus. "I will bring you food. But you have to stay here and be quiet while I'm in class. My mother would *not* approve of a monster invading her attic. Besides, I need time to figure out what to do with you."

Icicle turned his back, sniffling and squinting as his gaze circled the room. Rilla hoped he wasn't planning on getting into things or making a mess.

Clank, clank, clank!

That was her mom, banging a spoon on the water pipe that ran from the kitchen straight to the attic. It meant "Get down here this instant!"

"Coming, Sparrow!" Rilla hollered, even though she was too far away to be heard. (She called her mom by name so "Daughter would see Mother as Friend and not Authority Figure." Or so her mother said.

Sparrow *also* insisted she drop the "aunt" from Aunt Poppy for the same reason, but Rilla *liked* saying "aunt" because that's what *normal* kids from *normal* families said.)

Rushing about, she gathered her books and notes for morning classes. Home-schooling came in handy on days like this—no bus to miss or tardy slip to fetch from the office for being late. Of course, she *did* have to follow her mother's strict schedule.

"I'll be right back with breakfast," Rilla promised, wondering if she was crazy for leaving Icicle alone in her attic—but she had no choice.

"Having a monster for a pet will be *fun*," she added in a chipper voice, saying it more to convince herself than him.

He sniffed in an exasperated manner and returned to his nap position. From a distance, he was hard to spot among the surrounding animals. (Only the others weren't monsters and they never batted her hand away.)

Rilla locked the door, then took the back stairway to the kitchen. In the old days it had served as the servants' stairway, leading from the upstairs rooms to their live-in quarters behind the kitchen. Sparrow had turned the area into Rilla's classroom.

The walls displayed maps of the world, the solar system, and posters of multicultural kids. A computer hummed in one corner. Light from a giant aquarium cast a wavy glow on the wall.

On a long table sat cages intended for animals on loan from Sparrow's many sources—or from the backyard. Sparrow believed it was unnatural to keep living things in cages, so Rilla's classroom creatures were constantly returned—or freed.

Today, visitors included two rabbits on loan from a neighbor, and a garter snake Aunt Poppy's Ride-a-Mower had flushed from the yard last fall. Sparrow planned to set it free as soon as spring arrived.

Rilla liked having school here, but sometimes she missed her class back at Pickering Elementary. Sparrow believed "All the world is one's teacher" and "Students excel when not confined to one room all day."

Rilla's classes were held inside, outside, and all over the countryside—wherever Sparrow found the best setting for whatever she was teaching.

Once, she lectured on Admiral Byrd's expeditions to Antarctica from the top of a nearby mountain in the middle of a November blizzard to give Rilla the feel of surviving in sub-zero weather.

Rilla wished her mom believed in *community* home schooling. Six other former Pickering students met to study together, but she joined them only for field trips and special events.

That's how she'd met Joshua Banks (her one true love) and found out where he lived. (Up the street in the old Zanovick place.)

She liked the others in the group: Wally, Andrew, Marcia, and Kelly. Everyone except Tina Welter. She didn't like Tina for four reasons:

1. Rilla suspected Tina liked Joshua Banks too (which explained the snippy treatment Tina always gave her).

2. She'd never forgiven Tina for her gift of animal crackers at a third-grade party. Rilla had almost finished eating them before she realized Tina had bitten off all the heads and put the bodies back into the box.

3. Tina never missed an opportunity to point out the Earth family quirkiness.

4. Tina seemed to think it was hilarious to tack a "Gor" in front of Rilla's name.

"*N.F.*," Rilla would growl at her. "Not funny."

"Where've you been?" Sparrow grumbled, setting a plate of steamed rice on the round oak table in the middle of the room. She wore a ski sweater over her pajamas because it was always cold in this room.

Rilla hoped her mother would get dressed before the B & B guests came down to the breakfast Aunt Poppy was setting out in the dining room.

José was already there. She could hear him drumming on the table, trying out one of his new songs on her aunt.

Rilla took a seat and sipped her grapefruit juice. "Whoops!" She slapped a hand to her head, feigning forgetfulness. "I left my homework in the attic." (It wasn't a fib—she'd left it on purpose.) "I'll be right back."

Sparrow crinkled an eyebrow as she adjusted a barrette in her hair, which wasn't quite as long as Aunt Poppy's. "Well, hurry then," she said. "Your breakfast will be cold."

Rilla stopped in the kitchen and opened the freezer. She pulled out a carton of Holistic Double Dutch Chocolate Frozen Yogurt and a can of all-natural frozen lemonade.

There were no Popsicles in the Earths' freezer in the middle of January. And the only ones there in summer were homemade with fruit juice and no sugar. The monster would have to do without Popsicles until she could buy some at Mr. Baca's One-Stop Shoppette.

Grabbing a spoon and two bowls, Rilla peeked into the dining room to make sure Aunt Poppy was occupied. Yes. She was serving breakfast to a honeymooning couple from Tennessee while she talked (flirted?) with José.

Rilla hurried to the attic. Venturing inside, she juggled her arm load, unsure of what she might find.

What she *didn't* find was Icicle's face among the other fuzzy faces staring at her from the bed.

She glanced around the room. There he was, perched upon a pillow in her rocking chair. A shaft of morning light gleamed through the east window, reflecting brightly off his silvery coat. Rilla suddenly made the connection between Icicle's name, the color of his fur, and the month he represented.

He'd yanked a pile of books from her shelf, scattering them across the floor. Ignoring her, he rocked back and forth, intently reading *Where the Wild Things Are.*

Rilla knelt, setting the bowls on a braided rug. She dumped the entire carton of frozen yogurt into one and squeezed the lemonade from its cardboard can into the other.

"Here," she said. "Eat."

Seven eyes peered over the top of the book with an expression that said, *You've got to be kidding.* A sharp claw gave an indignant tap on the tabletop next to the rocking chair.

"Oh, right," Rilla muttered. She moved the bowls to the table. "I should have guessed it beneath you to eat off the floor like a dog."

He disappeared behind the book, dismissing her.

Rilla threw the empty cartons into the trash and rinsed her hands in the bathroom sink. She was beginning to feel a bit like a grumpy monster herself.

As she grabbed her homework and hurried down-stairs, worries began to trouble her mind.

Worries like: *What if the monster makes noises and disturbs the B & B guests?*

What if I haven't given him enough food? What if he eats my stuffed-animal collection?

What if Sparrow and Aunt Poppy discover him? What if he eats THEM?

Rilla gulped at the thought. Was he dangerous? He *is* a monster, she reminded herself. *What if, in the middle of a dark, spooky night, while I'm asleep, he. . . .*

Stop! she scolded herself, wishing she hadn't just read a book called *Vanished! Eleven Stories of Unexplained Disappearances.*

One more "what if" made Rilla shudder:

What if *she* became Unexplained Disappearance number twelve?

3

Why Not Leprechauns?

Earth wasn't Rilla's real last name. It used to be *Pinowski* before her mother and aunt went to court and legally changed it to something more—well—earthy. They told the judge, "We are all children of the earth. This name should belong to everyone."

The judge did not seem to agree or understand, but she okayed the change anyway for legal purposes.

The whole thing would've embarrassed Rilla to death if it'd happened now, but at the time she was only three, so she'd grown up an Earth.

Rilla's mom used to be Donna Knox—*after* she'd taken back her maiden name and *before* she'd become Sparrow Harmony Earth.

Aunt Poppy used to be Sally Street. That was her final last name after being married four times. Her full name was Sally Knox Bailey Hailey Hobbs Street.

Rilla didn't remember ever calling her Aunt Sally, but she thought having so many names—and ex-husbands—was funny.

Her *own* name, Rilla, came from a guru her mother once followed when she was younger. It meant "sisterhood" in some dead language.

Having a name other than the one she was born with worried Rilla every time she thought about her father. What if he tried to find her, but couldn't because he didn't know about the name change? (He left before she was born, so she never knew him.)

Rilla pictured her father wandering the streets of some faraway city, distraught over his failure to locate one R. Pinowski (or D. Knox) after long searches through piles of telephone books at the library.

Did he wonder what she looked like? (She didn't look like Sparrow, so she *must* resemble her father.) Was he responsible for the bony bump on her nose and her too-full lips?

Did he wonder if she'd inherited his sense of humor? Did he keep all his favorite things in a cookie tin too? Would he know every single word to "I'll Love You Till My Pickup's Lost Its Shine"?

One more question lingered in Rilla's mind, haunting her more than the others: *What if her father had no intention of finding her at all?*

• • •

During her morning break in lessons (equivalent to recess) Rilla *usually* went out to the barn to feed the kittens and play with them. But today she flew directly to the attic to check on Icicle.

He was still in the rocker, asleep under the cover of an open book (*There's a Monster in My Closet*).

Rilla was glad he wasn't doing all the horrible things she'd imagined him doing. Let him sleep. A sleeping monster was an out-of-trouble monster.

Her bed was still covered with treasures from her cookie tin. She pulled out a few others:

- the cork from her grandparents' fiftieth-anniversary champagne bottle

- Japanese yen from her second-grade pen pal who lived in Osaka

- a crinkled picture of her father (too distant and blurred to solve the bony nose bump and full lip mystery)

- her pink beaded baby bracelet, which read: GIRL PINOWSKI

Rilla packed away her treasures one by one, stopping to reread Mr. Tamerow's last postcard, mailed from Easter Island.

It said he looked forward to his next visit to the B & B, because "staying at Harmony House is better than staying with ten pampering grandmothers in any corner of the globe."

Maybe the B & B was better because guests were greeted with cups of steaming hot cocoa in winter, iced mango tea in summer, then given fuzzy slippers and plush white robes with HHB&B embroidered in cranberry letters. The Earth sisters liked to make visitors feel welcome.

Rilla returned the cookie tin to its special spot in the dresser, then tiptoed out the door. She hoped guests in the rooms at the bottom of the stairs didn't complain about unidentifiable snores coming from the attic.

• • •

In the afternoon Rilla snitched a berry bran muffin left over from breakfast. Nibbling it, she turned a page in the book she was reading for this week's book review. The story was about a boy with a dragon for a pet. Ha! *She* had a *monster* for a pet. *She* should be in a book.

"I'm returning your final exam on Ireland," Sparrow said, handing her the test paper. A half-rainbow sticker decorated the top.

Sparrow didn't believe in letter grades. Two rainbows meant *perfect.* One meant *excellent,* and a half-rainbow, *good.* Descending opinions were represented by lemons, liver, or moldy pizza. The equivalent of *F* was a bucket of soap suds.

"Good job," her mom continued. "Two mistakes. Leprechauns are mythical; they don't really exist. And Ireland's nickname is the Emerald Isle, not Sapphire Isle."

"Oh." Rilla spotted the frowning faces penciled next to her wrong answers. "Are you sure about leprechauns?" She really *wanted* to believe in them. If monsters could exist, why not leprechauns?

"Yes, I'm sure." Sparrow shoved wire-framed glasses onto her nose, then flipped through a world atlas. "We're finished with Ireland. Have you decided which country you want to study next?"

"Mmm." Rilla finished the muffin and pushed away her plate. "How about Botswana?"

Sparrow peered at Rilla over the top of her glasses. "Botswana?" She acted surprised, then pleased. "Fine. It's been a while since we studied an African country." After flipping to the index, she opened the atlas to the proper page. Then she stood up to point out Botswana on the world map, which took up most of one wall.

"Botswana is in the center of Africa, near the southern tip," her mother said. "And the language spoken is—"

"English?"

"How'd you know?"

Rilla grimaced. "Lucky guess."

"Very good." Her mom read on. "They also speak a language called Setswana."

Rilla wondered if her monster understood both languages.

"Okay, Botswana it is." Sparrow set the atlas aside. "Open your assignment book."

Rilla obeyed, groaning inside. All she wanted to know about Botswana was: How had the country produced Icicle? Were there others like him back home? Could somebody in Gaborone give her advice on how to take care of a grumpy monster?

Yet she had a feeling she was about to learn more than she ever wanted to know about the country.

". . . written report," her mom was saying. "A hands-on project you can build, a little about their history, music, traditions."

She paused while Rilla jotted down instructions. "You can turn everything in when you're ready." (Sparrow never gave her deadlines because they "didn't foster self-discipline.")

Rilla finished writing the assignment in her notebook.

Underneath, she scribbled a note to herself:

1. Ride bike to store.

2. Buy frozen yogurt, Popsicles, and lemonade.

3. Smuggle monster food to attic ASAP.

Biodegradable Names

"Come on, Pepsi."

Rilla coaxed the orange kitten along as she walked to the mailbox. Today was Saturday, so she took her time, enjoying sunshine after a week of cloudy gloom.

The kitten scampered down the sidewalk, dodging mounds of mushy snow. Pepsi wasn't his "official" name. He didn't have one. Sparrow believed "naming animals limits them from all nature intends them to be."

Rilla didn't always agree with her mom's philosophies. That's why she'd secretly given names to the kittens—on a day when she was *really* angry at her mom.

It was last Halloween, and the home-schoolers had gathered at Joshua Banks's house for a party. Rilla was so jazzed about going to Joshua's house, she was downright giddy.

Then, *in front of everybody,* Sparrow made her return all the Halloween treats everyone had given her. Rilla's giddy mood had bungee-jumped to resentment.

At home she'd gone straight to the barn and given "treat" names to the kittens—who were only a few days old. Besides Pepsi, there was Milk Dud, Dorito, and the mama cat, Oreo.

Soda and junk food were forbidden at Harmony House. Rilla wished Sparrow would occasionally bend the rules.

One time when she was riding bikes with Marcia and Kelly, they stopped for burgers and fries and Cokes. Rilla stuffed herself, loving every bite. When she got home, she had to feign hunger and force down a bowl of tofu casserole—or risk a lecture from Sparrow.

Rilla clicked her tongue at Pepsi, urging him to keep up with her.

Arriving at the mailbox, she paused to give the tag-along cat a good scratching. Then she opened the Earths' box and dropped mail into the cloth bag.

Behind her, a bike skidded to a stop. It was Tina, coming to collect the Welters' mail.

The windy ride made Tina's spiky hair stick up like a frightened surfer's. She was dressed in a warm-up ski outfit (periwinkle and rose) with matching snap-ins on her athletic shoes.

Rilla wore sweatpants (navy), a sweatshirt (green and orange), and standard Keds (red). Okay, she was terribly mismatched colorwise. *So what?* she told herself. *So what.*

"Here, kitty," Tina called, hopping off the bike to scoop Pepsi into her arms. "Are you a stray?"

"No, he isn't," Rilla answered.

Tina acknowledged Rilla's presence with a blank look. "I wasn't talking to you; I was talking to the kitten."

"Did you expect a reply?" *Good answer, Rilla.* She smiled at her own cleverness.

Tina ignored the comment. "Is he yours?"

A surge of protectiveness washed over Rilla. If Tina tried to steal Pepsi, she'd tackle her, bicycle and all. "Yes, he's mine."

At least Tina didn't ask the kitten's name.

"So what's his name?"

Rilla sighed, closing the mailbox and locking it. "Pepsi."

"What a dumb name for a cat." Tina gave a disgusted laugh. "Do you know how to spell it?"

"What do you mean?"

"Well, your mother doesn't know how to spell. I figured you don't either, since she's schooling you."

Rilla bristled at the jab about her family. "What do you mean?"

"Look at the sign on your house," Tina said. " 'Peace to Every One.' Your mom doesn't even know *everyone* is one word, not two."

"Yes she does." Rilla was tempted to snatch Pepsi from Tina's arms and bolt down the street so she wouldn't have to explain one of Sparrow's far-out theories. "My mother spelled it that way on purpose."

It was Tina's turn to ask "What do you mean?"

Rilla hated being forced to defend her family's strange ways. "It's spelled as two words because the actions of *one* are equally important as the actions of *every* one, so the words stand alone." (At least that's what Sparrow had told her.)

"How stupid." Tina wrinkled her nose. "Wait till I tell Joshua."

Rilla's face turned hot and cold at the same time. She never would've tried to explain Sparrow's quirks if she had known Tina planned to have a good chuckle over it later with Joshua Banks.

Rilla snatched the cat from Tina's grasp.

Tina let her take him. "Leave it to your bird-mother to come up with something *that* strange," she scoffed, throwing one leg over the bar on her bike. "Your weirdo bird-mother *and* your flower-aunt."

Rilla jogged home, clutching the kitten and mail bag to her chest.

The anger misting her eyes wasn't even directed at Tina. Rilla knew she was an easy target. (Who wouldn't be with a name like hers?)

Instead, her bitter tears were directed at those who'd *made* her such an easy target—her weirdo bird-mother and her flower-aunt.

5

King of the Attic

"Where are you taking the ice chest?"

Rilla jumped. With all the noise coming from the washer and dryer, she hadn't heard Aunt Poppy clunking down the basement steps in her queen-sized earth shoes. She wore standard cleaning clothes, complete with her ozone-layer T-shirt. (It had a big hole in the middle.)

"Um, I'm taking the ice chest to the attic," Rilla told her, balancing it on one knee to get a better grip.

"Why?"

"Um, so I can have cold drinks in my room while I'm doing homework." *Quick thinking, Rilla.* "It's too far to run down three flights of stairs to the kitchen every time I get thirsty."

She felt pleased with her answer. The *real* reason, of course, was to keep Icicle's frozen treats handy.

"You'll still have to haul ice upstairs, and we need all the ice we can make for our guests."

The clothes dryer buzzed. Aunt Poppy opened the

door. The lemony smell of fabric softener whooshed into the basement air.

"Um, I'll leave plenty for the guests," Rilla told her. "I promise."

"Well, okay." Aunt Poppy began folding towels on a long table. The laundry traveled from the basement to the guest rooms, then back again. A never-ending cycle.

Rilla headed for the stairs.

"Wait," her aunt called.

"Yeah?" Had she changed her mind?

"Please don't start every sentence with 'Um.' "

"Oh, um, okay."

Aunt Poppy playfully snapped a hand towel at her.

Rilla struggled up the steps with the cooler, stopping every few feet to rest, and once to say good-bye to José, who was checking out today.

A pang of sadness rippled through Rilla when he gave her a wink and a wave before disappearing down the stairs with his bag and guitar case.

Living in a bed and breakfast was difficult some-times—not being able to run or make noise inside her own house; watching everything she did and said in front of guests.

Worse was having people come and go in her life. Constantly.

One-nighters, as Aunt Poppy called them, didn't matter much; Rilla knew she'd never see them again.

But the ones who always returned, like José and Mr. Tamerow, those were the hardest good-byes of all—mainly because Rilla had to act as though their leaving didn't bother her.

And it *did*. Every time she got used to having them around, they'd up and disappear. Sometimes she'd say good-bye, then run to the attic and curl up in her quilt to cry. And no one ever knew.

Watching people leave was hard on a person's heart.

Rilla hoisted the ice chest and started off again. She hadn't meant for her father to pop into her mind at that particular moment, but he did.

Huffing, she hurried all the way to the attic without stopping again, as if that would keep the loneliness from catching up with her.

• • •

When Rilla opened the attic door, Icicle was *not* in the rocking chair or on the bed.

Panic flittered inside her stomach.

She kerplopped the ice chest in a corner, then went on a monster hunt.

He wasn't under the bed, in her closet, or on top of the bookshelves.

Next she tried the bathroom.

There he was, relaxing in the tub, up to his scraggly chin in bubbles.

The room smelled of lilacs. He'd borrowed the bub-

ble bath Sparrow had given her for Christmas. The nerve!

"Stop pretending you were invited here. You weren't."

He blew a paw full of bubbles across the bathroom.

Rilla tsk-sighed. "You act as though you're King of the Attic. I suppose you want me to bow and address you as King Icicle."

He raised a hairy eyebrow, as if considering the suggestion.

She straightened the bath mat. "Look, I'm leaving now—off to the store to buy more food for you, Your Royal Highness. What you ate last night was supposed to last for a week.

"You could at least pretend to be grateful," she added. "Or smile. Or say thank you. *Or* ask what *you* can do for *me.*"

Why couldn't the monster be like the kittens? Taking care of them was work too, but at least they rewarded her with entertaining stunts, soft nuzzles, and purrs of appreciation. Not with silent demands or insulting looks. And they never took things that didn't belong to them.

Icicle reached for something on the shelf next to the tub. Her earphones! He'd borrowed her Walkman, too!

Slipping them over his head, the monster sank lower in the bubbles, closed all seven eyes, and smiled slightly, revealing his pointy fangs. Rilla thought she heard humming.

She left him there, slamming the door on her way out.

What else could she do? Pull the plug and hope he swirled down the drain? All the way back to Botswana?

• • •

For the next few weeks, most of Rilla's savings went toward frozen yogurt, Popsicles, and lemonade.

The home-schoolers' Charity Project required a dollar-a-week donation from each student—which hadn't been a problem before Icicle and his hearty appetite moved in. Well, she'd have to fudge on donations for a few weeks until she solved her monster problem.

Meanwhile, Icicle rearranged the attic, building a fortress in the northwest corner with stacks of books, an overturned chair, shoe boxes, and the ice chest.

He kept quiet all day, mainly because he was sleeping. But every night after his bath (part of her allowance kept him in bubble bath, too) he arranged himself inside his fortress—on a pillow atop the rocking chair—and read.

He loved the poems in *Monster Soup* (if reading them over and over was any indication). He dog-eared pages in *The Book of Three* where the monster, Gurgi, appeared. He underlined Grendel's name in Sparrow's copy of *Beowulf*. And each time he read the end of *Frankenstein,* he wept tiny purple tears.

Sometimes he kept Rilla awake with irritating monster noises—sniffling and snickering, sneezing and wheezing. Plus, he took it upon himself to borrow her King Kong reading lamp from her nightstand.

One night Rilla hunched under the covers, glaring at Icicle, wishing she had her reading lamp back so she could finish her library book on Botswana.

She remembered how freaked she'd been the first day Icicle arrived, and how scared she was to leave him alone in the attic. If Sparrow hadn't harped at her about how "all life is worthy of our trust and respect," she probably would've locked Icicle in the linen closet the first day.

Yet she'd trusted him to stay put and keep quiet—
and he had. She only wished he'd turned out to be
playful and affectionate—qualities much easier to love
than his grumpiness.

At first she'd even imagined herself taking Icicle for
long winter walks on a leash—and bumping into
Joshua Banks, her one true love.

"Wow," Joshua would exclaim, raising his shoulders and shoving his fingertips into his jean pockets
the cute way he did. "You have a pet monster?"

She would nod, a bit shyly. "Why, yes," she'd say.
"This is Icicle, my loving monster pet. I'm teaching
him tricks. Like how to read books and build
fortresses and take bubble baths."

"Cool," Joshua would say. "Can I come to your
house? Can I see where you keep him?"

"Sure," she would answer. "Would you like to stay
for dinner? Would you like to be my boyfriend?"

Then Tina Welter would saunter by and see the two
of them laughing together, sharing secrets, holding
hands. While an adoring Icicle led the way. And Tina
would be so jealous, all the spikes in her hair would
fall flat.

• • •

The annoying slurps of a sleepy monster drinking
iced lemonade made Rilla's daydream pop—like lilac
bubbles in the tub. The absurdity of the sight brought
her back to reality.

She could never let Joshua Banks meet Icicle.

Any kind of monster—not to mention a rude and cranky one—would only add to Joshua's perception of the Earth family as abnormal. (How many *normal* families kept monsters for pets?)

Ah, no. Rilla closed her eyes, sighing. Her little secret must remain in the attic—meaning she was doomed to keeping the January monster all to herself.

Monster Talk

On the first day of February, a second box arrived in the mail.

Maybe it's a return mailer, Rilla told herself, *with a note saying, "There's been a mistake. Please return the January Selection at once."*

But when she picked up the box, shifting weight told her it was occupied. The back of her neck began to sweat in spite of the frigid air.

She squinted at the colorful foreign stamps, then at the return address:

M.O.T.M. Club
Wellington, New Zealand

New Zealand? "Wow," Rilla whispered to a box that was heavier than the one from Botswana. "*This* package came from a different country. Monsters must be *everywhere*."

Striding back to the house, she held the box steady, careful not to jiggle it too much. A second angry monster was not what she'd ordered. Of course, she hadn't *ordered* any monsters at all.

Someone else had. But who? And why?

Rilla had hashed over possible suspects a zillion times, even considering the whole thing a prank from Tina Welter—or another kind of weird lesson, staged by her mother.

Surely *somebody* would confess sooner or later. . . .

Racing upstairs, Rilla headed straight for the attic before Sparrow or Aunt Poppy could ask what had come in the mail.

She hadn't made her bed yet, so she smoothed the rumpled quilt before setting down the package. This one wasn't wiggling and bulging in an angry sort of way, like Icicle's box had. Good sign? Or bad?

Rilla glowered at the package. Maybe if she ignored the box, it would go away. Disappear. Beam itself back to New Zealand.

And if it worked, she'd try it on Tina Welter—ha! She imagined Tina waking up in New Zealand surrounded by monsters—all wearing periwinkle and rose warm-ups, just like hers.

You're stalling, Rilla.

I know.

Open the box.

Rilla picked it up, reluctant to release whatever was

inside. Icicle was a royal pain in the toe. How could she handle *another* monster in her attic?

She felt a tug on the quilt. Icicle was climbing up to investigate. The water bed undulated with his quick movements. He sniffle-snorted around the package, then began to whine in anticipation.

Aha. *Maybe all he needs is a friend to change his attitude. Then he might stop being such a creepy monster.* (Creep as in *jerk,* not as in *scary.*)

With the same enthusiasm she felt whenever Sparrow made her pick out unbleached cotton underwear from the Nature Undies catalog, Rilla unpeeled the mailing tape, partially opening one end of the box.

Scrambling from the bed, she flattened herself against a far wall and waited.

What emerged from the package was *not* what she had expected. What she had expected was a copy of Icicle.

But the monster who tumbled out was pink from head to claw. It stood tall, smoothing and patting its fur into place A pink bow circled a pudgy neck. Hanging to a poochy belly from a pink ribbon was a pink heart.

Once the monster had arranged itself, a paw with pink polished claws politely handed Rilla the enclosed card.

Edging closer, Rilla grasped it with a nod and a "Thank you very much." It read:

Monster of the Month Club
—

February Selection

Name: Sweetie Pie   *Gender:* Female

Homeland: New Zealand

Likes: Pink bubble gum, flowers (pink only),

pink fruit punch

Doesn't like to be alone.

"Sweetie Pie?" Rilla knelt to peer closely at the new arrival.

The monster chittered a bit, staying at attention as if she knew Rilla wanted to look her over—and would be quite pleased with what she saw.

Then she gave a little twirl on one paw, showing off.

The February monster was plump, twice as roly-poly as Icicle, with a pug nose, pug ears, and long curly lashes. (This one came with two eyes.) Her tail spiraled like a pig's, a pink ribbon twined around it.

If monsters could be labeled cute, she was a whole lot cuter than monster number one.

Rilla stroked her fur. Sweetie Pie gave a sigh, snuggling against Rilla's hand. *Oh, good, she'll let me pet her.*

Meanwhile, Icicle teetered on the edge of the bed, all seven eyes cemented on Sweetie Pie. What was ailing him? Was he allergic to pink?

Rilla touched him. He sprang from her reach, hopped across the bed, and landed next to their new guest, riding the water-bed waves like a surfer hanging eight. (That's how many toes he had.)

Icicle clucked a few strange noises to Sweetie Pie. Monster talk? He patted her pink fur.

In a heartbeat Sweetie Pie whirled, whacking him so hard with the back of her paw, he tumbled off the bed and flumped to the floor.

Sweetie Pie gazed at Rilla as if nothing odd had just happened.

A bewildered Icicle, too stunned to move, gawked dizzily up at the pink monster.

Rilla swallowed a laugh. *Now* she knew what was wrong with him. Grumpy ol' Icicle had fallen in love!

The Pink Fortress

Rilla gathered her things for school—a hard task with Sweetie Pie dogging her every step.

"Can't you take a nap?" she asked, trying not to sound annoyed. "Or read a book?" She'd hoped Icicle might entertain their new guest, but he'd retreated to his fortress to nurse his pride after Sweetie Pie whomped him.

The pink monster clung to Rilla's leg, chortling with love.

Rilla grabbed the Matterhorn sweatshirt Mr. Tamerow had brought her from his trip to Switzerland. "I can't play with you," she told Sweetie Pie. "I have school."

As she pulled the sweatshirt over her head, Rilla remembered what Icicle had done as soon as he arrived—built himself a fortress. "Ah, maybe *that's* what you need. A home of your own."

After stacking her schoolbooks by the door, Rilla dragged a wicker towel cabinet from the bathroom to the southeast corner of the attic, as far from Icicle as possible. Positioning the cabinet on its side, connecting her desk and dresser, she blocked off a four-by-four area.

The bath mat was pink and shaggy. Rilla smoothed it onto the floor inside the area, then draped pink towels over the cabinet so the monster would be surrounded with her favorite color.

The corner looked as if it had been colored by a giant pink crayon.

Rilla tossed in a few stuffed animals, pink, of course, and moved her bedside radio to the desk. Twirling the dial, she set it on the station that played love songs day and night—assuming the Valentine-month monster would like that.

Rilla turned the volume low so the music wouldn't bother Icicle, who pretended to nap even though three of his eyes stayed open, watching.

Lifting Sweetie Pie, Rilla cuddled her. "I'll bring you food during my break," she promised, setting the monster inside her little home. "Meanwhile, please stay here and be quiet. And don't fight with Icicle."

Grabbing her books, Rilla moved to the door, glancing back to admire her handiwork.

Sweetie Pie stood frozen. Panic paled her pink face. In one leap she bounded over the desk and waddle-raced to the door, chitter-pleading with Rilla not to leave.

"I have to." Rilla stroked the monster's fuzzy head

to calm her. "I'll be back soon," she cooed. "Icicle will keep you company."

At the mention of his name, Icicle opened the other four eyes, honoring Sweetie Pie with an ornery grin. One eyebrow wiggled up and down a few times; fangs glinted white in the morning sun.

Giving a disinterested sniff, Sweetie Pie returned her attention to Rilla, who was squeezing out the door to keep her newest pet from following.

The forlorn look in the pink monster's eyes almost broke Rilla's heart.

• • •

Sparrow tapped a pencil on the table to get her daughter's attention. "Am I boring you?" They were in the middle of an oral quiz on Botswana.

"Why?" Rilla's neck warmed. Had she given a wrong answer without thinking? Had she said Botswana's flag was blue with a *pink* stripe instead of blue with a *black* stripe?

"I'm tired of repeating every question."

"Sorry." Rilla lowered her gaze. "I've got something on my mind."

Sparrow yanked off her glasses. "Joshua Banks again?"

"No-o-o." How did mothers *know* stuff like that?

"Anything you want to talk about?" Sparrow sipped guava juice from her Vanishing Rain Forest mug.

"Nope."

Aunt Poppy appeared at the classroom door. Today her hair hung in a long braid over one shoulder to keep it out of the way while she cleaned. "Rill, did you take a kitten to the attic?"

"No, ma'am." Kittens weren't allowed in the house in case guests were allergic.

"Hmm." Aunt Poppy yanked on her braid as if it helped her think. "The lady from Utah—the one in B-3—said she heard a baby crying in the room above her. The only room above her is the attic. I assured her it wasn't a baby."

Rilla's heart stalled. "Well, um, I left the radio on." She straightened in her chair. It wasn't a fib; she *had* left the radio on.

Sparrow smiled apologetically at Aunt Poppy. "Number five," she said, as if her quiz hadn't already been interrupted twice. "What's the capital of Botswana?"

"Gaborone," Rilla replied. *Home of King Icicle,* she added to herself.

"Correct." Sparrow penciled a happy face next to the question.

Rilla scrunched low in her seat. Was Sweetie Pie really crying? The card from the box said she didn't like to be alone.

"Number six," Sparrow continued. "What is Botswanan money called?"

She's not alone. She's got Icicle.

Icicle doesn't count; she ignores him.

Right. Rilla agreed with the voice inside her head. *Yet what am I supposed to do? Stay with her all day and night? Bring her to school?*

Impossible.

"Pass?"

"Huh?"

"Earth to Earth. Come in, please." Sparrow sat back and crossed her arms, irritated. "If you don't know the answer, say *pass* and I'll come back to it."

"I *do* know the answer."

"Well, would you care to say it out loud, since this is an *oral* exam?"

Rilla squirmed under her mother's scrutiny. *Better act normal so she doesn't suspect anything.* "Botswanan money is called *pula.*"

"Correct." Sparrow drew another happy face next to the question. "Number—"

"And," Rilla continued. "*Pula* is also the Setswana word for *rain.* Rain is almost as important as money in Botswana because the country is part desert."

"Oh, really?" Sparrow placed one hand over her heart, acting shocked and amused at Rilla's extended answer.

"Not only that," Rilla added, "but one of the nicest things you can say to someone in Botswana is 'Let there be rain.' "

Sparrow scribbled a note to add extra credit to Rilla's monthly evaluation. "I've never seen you so interested in geography before."

Rilla shrugged. She'd read the Botswana book cover to cover, searching for information about Icicle's origin. Information that simply wasn't there.

"Let's see now; where were we?" Sparrow shuffled test papers in her Botswana folder. "Number seven. Name a few exports."

"Diamonds, cowpeas, and . . ." Rilla paused. "What are cowpeas?"

"Um." Sparrow acted flustered. "I don't know."

"But you're the *teacher*." Rilla mimicked Sparrow's shocked and amused stance. "You're supposed to know *everything*."

Her mother's laugh sounded guilty. Yet Rilla was thankful she was laughing instead of dashing upstairs to see what was crying in the attic.

"What else do they export?" Sparrow asked.

"Monsters."

"Ril-la." Her mother let the folder fall shut. "I guess that ends our test, if you're not going to be serious."

Rilla was tempted to say, *I am serious. Come, I'll show you.*

But Sparrow would either freak and call the Animal Protection Agency, *or* she'd adopt the monsters and teach them to love one another, live together in harmony, and drink home-squeezed guava juice instead of the quirky things they drank.

"Was that your final answer?"

"Nope. I *meant* to say copper and nickel."

"Correct."

Another penciled happy face.

And another close call.

Loves Music, Loves to Dance

"If you go outside, please feed the kittens," Sparrow said, dismissing Rilla after classes were finished for the day.

She *was* planning on going outside—to search the yard for any spring flowers pushing their tips through the muddy earth.

It might be too early, but winter had been mild. Last year, flowers started sprouting by mid-February, although Rilla couldn't remember any being pink.

She was also wracking her brain, trying to recall information about New Zealand, home of the new monster. It was one of the first countries she'd studied after Sparrow had started home-schooling her.

Rilla remembered preparing a "New Zealand dinner" for Sparrow and Aunt Poppy as one of her assignments. (Baked kumaras—sweet potatoes—and toheroa soup, made from green clams that Mr. Baca at the One-Stop Shoppette had to special order.)

Rilla also remembered reading that New Zealand was the first country to give women the right to vote, which Sparrow had *loved*.

What she *didn't* remember reading was anything about pink monsters inhabiting New Zealand.

Rilla wandered to the backyard. The lady from Utah was sitting on the patio in the afternoon sun, covered from head to toe with long sleeves, long pants, gloves, and a floppy straw hat tied with a ribbon that matched a cluster of pink plastic sand plums nestled on the brim.

Waving at her, Rilla wondered why people bothered to sit in the sun all covered up.

She worked her way around the house, searching for green shoots peeking through the dirt. No luck. She even wandered up to the old Zanovick place to see if flowers there had started to bud.

And maybe see if Joshua Banks was out and about this afternoon.

He was nowhere in sight. A girl's bike lay on its side in the driveway. Tina Welter's?

Disgusted by thoughts of Joshua and Tina sharing math lessons, Rilla hurried back to the B & B, stopping at the barn to feed the kittens.

The barn remained a relic from the days when Harmony House was a farm. Plans had been made to tear it down before the Earths moved in, but Aunt Poppy rallied to save it, thinking it a perfect place to store things.

Now it served as a hiding spot for her Ride-a-Mower. Sparrow *hated* the clunky, ear-splitting, smelly machine.

Harmony House's original lawn mower had been a goat. Aunt Poppy named the goat Nancy after one of her ex-husbands' new wives. Nancy did a great job of keeping the grass trimmed; however, she *also* took it upon herself to chew up *everything* in the yard, like lawn chairs and toys and rugs hung out to air.

Then Nancy chewed holes in a few fences and ate her way through the neighbors' yards. After she chewed up a few pairs of shoes and made one family move because of her unfortunate odor, the neighbors signed a petition and Nancy found greener pastures on a farm east of town.

Before the grass had time to grow back, the Ride-a-Mower was delivered to Aunt Poppy from Mr. Tamerow in exchange for a week's stay at Harmony House. He'd gotten a great deal on it from a factory going out of business in Nutbush, Tennessee.

The mower represented everything Sparrow abhorred about *doing things in an unnatural fashion,* but Aunt Poppy loved it. Rilla figured what she loved was the sense of power it gave her—ruling the backyard from her high perch, like an army general on top of a tank.

Stepping around the mower, Rilla searched for the mama cat.

She found Oreo lying on her side in a spot of sun. The kits tumbled over each other to greet Rilla, meandering around her ankles, mewing for dinner. She filled their bowls with crunchies and fresh water from a jug, then paused to pet Dorito, her favorite, the feisty one.

"You guys are so easy to please," she muttered. "Why can't *you* live in my attic instead of monsters?"

Leaving the kittens full and content, Rilla returned to the house, taking the back stairs to the attic. She expected to find Sweetie Pie still at the door, weeping for her.

But the pink monster had cranked up the volume of the radio and was dancing to songs on a country-and-western station instead of the love-song station Rilla had picked.

Sweetie Pie was decked out in an old cowboy hat she'd found perched on top of Rilla's bedpost, a pink bandanna stolen from the neck of Hef, the stuffed cow, and a string of pink beads from Rilla's jewelry box. The beads, slung around the monster's pudgy neck, almost touched the floor as she step-step-kicked to the music.

Rilla laughed at Sweetie Pie's silliness. She grabbed the monster's paws, dancing the two step around the room. Sweetie Pie's chittering kept time to the music, almost as if she were singing.

When the song ended, Rilla flopped onto her bed,

huffing for air. The monster scrambled up beside her, bouncing a stuffed rabbit and mouse clean off the bed.

Icicle tried to act disgusted, grumble-clucking to himself, hairy arms stiffly folded across his belly. But the way he cocked one eyebrow over his sideways glance told Rilla he was dying to join them—only his crotchety reputation wouldn't allow it.

"I know what we can do next." Rilla scrambled off the bed to get her cookie tin from the dresser. "Since you like country music, I'll sing you my favorite song." She unfolded the words and handed them to Sweetie Pie, assuming this monster could read like Icicle.

She lowered the volume on the radio, then burrowed into the back of her closet to find the ukulele Mr. Tamerow had sent last year from Maui.

Rilla tuned the ukulele, strummed the intro to her song, and began:

"He called me from a truck stop in Albuquerque.
I screened it on my answering machine.
When I heard his voice, Lord I started cryin'.
Thought I'd never hear from that cheatin' man
again'."

The pink monster squealed, clapping her paws in rhythm. Rilla, pleased at Sweetie Pie's reaction, barreled on into the chorus:

"Oh-h-h-h, oh, Ok-la-ho-ma.
 You locked me up and throw'd away the key.
 Oh-h-h-h, oh, Ok-la-ho-ma.
 That wanderin' man'll be the end of me."

As she sang the words, Rilla's brain made the connection between the chorus of her favorite song and the home office of the Monster of the Month Club. *Gee, what a coincidence.*

Meanwhile, Sweetie Pie was bouncing higher and higher on the bed, almost causing a tidal wave as she clucked along with the beat.

" 'I'll love you till the redbuds stop their bloomin'.'
 A lie like that could melt this heart of mine.
 But the words that made me his alone forever:
 'I'll love you till my pickup's lost its shine.' "

"Oh-h-h-h, oh, Ok-la—"
"RILLA HARMONY EARTH!"
Sparrow's angry voice cut through the ukulele music like a machete.

9

Nightmare of the Month Club

"What are you doing up there?" Sparrow's voice was barely a shade from a shriek.

"Nothing!" Rilla called back.

"*Nothing?* It sounds like the roof's caving in. Come down here so I don't have to yell."

Sweetie Pie hadn't stopped when the music ended. She was still bouncing up and down on the bed, clapping her paws and clucking.

"Hush!" Rilla hissed, catching her in mid-bounce. How could she open the attic door without Sparrow seeing the monster?

"Did you hear me?" her mother yelled.

Rilla raced to the bathroom, depositing Sweetie Pie in the tub. She knew the monster wouldn't stay there, but by the time Miss Chunky climbed out and maneuvered the slippery doorknob with her paws, Rilla'd be out the attic door, locking it behind her.

Skipping down the stairs, she smiled at her mom, acting as if nothing strange had been going on.

Sparrow's eyebrows were touching, which immediately told Rilla she was *not* a happy mother. "Guests from Indiana just checked in to celebrate their thirtieth wedding anniversary. First thing they did was call downstairs to complain about the noise. I was too embarrassed to tell them it was my own daughter causing the ruckus."

"Sorry." Rilla *was* sorry, although she'd been having a terrific time, playing and singing for Sweetie Pie.

She *hated* the rules around here: Keep quiet. Walk, don't run. No pets in the house. No junk food. No fun. No fair.

Someday, when she had her own house, she would play her ukulele and sing at the top of her lungs whenever she felt like it. She'd run up and down the stairs and hallways for no reason at all. *And* she'd fill the fridge with goodies *not* found in Sparrow's *Garden of Eatin'* cookbook.

Sparrow leaned against the wall, pressing one finger to her lips as if she *really* wanted to say more, but was struggling not to. "I'm sorry I yelled." Her voice grappled for control. "I don't believe in it." (Yelling shriveled the inner self.)

But Rilla's inner self wasn't shriveling. It was bouncing between resentment at her mother's strictness— and amusement. (She found it hilarious whenever Sparrow slipped as *the perfect Earth Mother.*)

Rilla knew better than to laugh out loud, though. Earth Mothers might believe in killing their young. . . .

"I need a few things from the store," Sparrow said, changing the subject. "Will you go?"

"Sure." Rilla felt pleased. She was almost out of pink bubble gum. All she had left was Grape-a-Lot, which was purple, meaning the pink monster wouldn't touch it.

Plus, Sparrow always gave her extra money as a treat. Not spending her own allowance on flowers and bubble bath greatly appealed to her.

Sparrow fished money and a shopping list from her apron pocket, along with a letter. "This is addressed to you. Didn't you see it when you picked up the mail this morning?"

Rilla glanced at the postmark, hoping it wasn't another surprise from Oklahoma. Nope, it was from Alaska. *Whew!* The sight of Mr. Tamerow's familiar squiggly handwriting lit her up inside as much as singing her pickup-truck song.

"Yay!" Rilla cheered. "Is Mr. Tamerow coming to visit?"

"I don't read your mail." (Part of Sparrow's "privacy fosters trust" philosophy.)

Rilla raced back to the attic.

"Please keep the noise down," her mother called. "And hurry back from the store. I need the dandelion greens for dinner."

Beyond the attic door, muffled whimpers met her ears. Geez, what a *baby* the February Selection was.

Inside, Sweetie Pie stood tall in her fortress, dabbing

at her eyes with pink toilet paper, glaring at Rilla as if to say, *How could you leave me alone in a room full of white porcelain?*

Rilla stifled an urge to cuddle Sweetie Pie and zing her back to a party mood. Maybe if the monster pouted a while, Rilla'd have a few moments alone to read Mr. Tamerow's letter before she left for the store.

Rilla hoped he was writing to tell her he'd be coming soon to the B & B. She loved it when he visited her classroom as a "guest lecturer" (what Sparrow called him). He told nifty stories—like the one about riding the Orient Express through tunnels deep under the Alps.

Or staying in a lighthouse in Nova Scotia with a pet lobster named Bob.

Or watching a girls' swinging contest at spring festival time in Korea. (The girl who swung the highest, ringing a bell with her foot each time, won a prize.)

While Rilla searched her desk for a letter opener, Sweetie Pie climbed out of her fortress and wandered aimlessly around the attic, detouring Icicle's corner even though he was sleeping.

Rilla ignored her, which made the monster's injured feelings heal rather quickly.

Climbing onto the desk, Sweetie Pie peered over Rilla's shoulder as she unfolded Mr. Tamerow's letter. They read together in silence:

Dear Rilly [what Mr. Tamerow called her],

Next stop: Harmony House B & B. Tell Poppy to get my room ready. Have lots of new stories to tell you about my latest trip (to Alaska). Miss you! See you soon! XXXOOO!

Mr. T. [what she called him]

"He's coming!" Rilla's unexpected shout made Sweetie Pie slip off the desk and tumble to the floor. Rolling upright, she gave an embarrassed giggle-cluck.

An impending visit from Mr. Tamerow always made Rilla excited—especially today. Mr. T. knew more than anyone in the whole world—except maybe Ms. Noir at the library, who'd helped Rilla find books on Botswana. (She even knew what cowpeas were—just another name for black-eyed peas.)

Surely Mr. Tamerow would know about monsters around the globe, wouldn't he? Maybe he'd explain it all to her and tell her what to do with Icicle and Sweetie Pie.

Rilla folded the letter and put it away in the cookie tin, along with the pickup-truck song. Sweetie Pie had helped herself to Rilla's stash of stamps from Botswana and New Zealand, torn from the monster boxes. She was licking them and trying to make them stick to her tummy.

Grabbing Edward Elephant off the bed, Rilla hugged him to her chest. What advice would Mr. Tamerow give her? She squinted at a slumbering Icicle, thinking. Maybe he'd tell her to write to Oklahoma and ask them to cancel her subscription in the Monster of the Month Club.

Two monsters were a handful. How long could she keep them a secret? What if they grew larger? Bigger than the attic?

What if they escaped? What if they held the lady from Utah hostage and tormented her?

And, worst of all, what if Oklahoma *couldn't* cancel her subscription, and the monsters kept coming and coming and *coming*?

Yikes.

Rilla made up her mind. She'd write to Oklahoma. As soon as she got home from the store. Before her Monster of the Month Club turned into the *Nightmare* of the Month Club . . .

10

A Flower, a Wad of Pink Bubble Gum, and Thou

"You have the luckiest mother in the world."

Mr. Baca's son, Carlos, peered at Rilla through the display glass of the fresh flower case in Mr. Baca's One-Stop Shoppette. The glass made his eyes look unnaturally large, like fish eyes.

"Excuse me?" Rilla said.

Carlos removed a carnation, then straightened, closing the door. "I mean, you've bought your mother a pink flower every day this month. For Valentine's Day, I assume. What a nifty idea; wish I'd thought of it. My girlfriend would be so impressed."

Rilla watched Carlos wrap the flower in green tissue paper. She didn't offer to explain that her mother never *saw* the flowers.

That, in fact, his precious flowers were *eaten*.

By a monster.

Who spit out the stringy green stems.

Nor did she offer to explain that she was *forced* to

buy a fresh flower every day because picky Sweetie Pie wouldn't nibble—wouldn't even *touch*—one that looked as if it were *thinking* of wilting.

The monster preferred roses, but at $1.49 each, Rilla quickly switched to carnations at 50 cents apiece. Still, she was slowly going broke.

Carlos handed her the flower. He'd wrapped it so the chilly trip home wouldn't brown the edges of the petals. "What else can I get you?"

"That's all." Rilla tossed the carnation into a hand basket, next to a supply of lemonade, frozen yogurt, Popsicles, bubble gum, fruit punch, and bubble bath.

"Do you plan on buying flowers the rest of February?" Carlos asked. "Or just until Valentine's Day?"

Rilla chuckled, stepping toward the vegetable department to search for dandelion greens. "Haven't decided," she called back. "Might keep it up all year."

"Wow." Carlos seemed impressed as he waved good-bye.

When she finished shopping, Rilla stopped at the card counter. Carlos's comments reminded her that Valentine's Day was approaching. Should she buy a card for Joshua Banks? Would he buy one for her?

She read every pink and red and lacy card on the rack. None was right. Most were far too mushy— which should have been okay, since Joshua Banks was her one true love. Yet it'd be *more* okay if he *knew* he was her one true love. Or, better yet, if he knew *she* was *his*.

Love could be so complicated.

Well, she'd just have to create an original valentine for him. Two, rather. One she could sign, and one, extra mushy, to send anonymously.

She hoped Sweetie Pie hadn't used up all her pink crayons. They'd been worn down to nubs last time the monster had the urge to color.

Rilla packed groceries into her backpack, snitching a wad of pink bubble gum from the stash she'd bought for Sweetie Pie. Climbing onto her bike, she waited for her jaw to soften the gum before shoving off.

The sudden *clackety-clack* of skateboard wheels made her whirl around. Joshua Banks sailed toward her, arms out to steady himself, grinning a grin meant just for her. His smile showed both dimples.

Joshua was the only person Rilla knew who had dimples carved in both cheeks. Mr. Tamerow had a chin dimple, and José sported one in his left cheek. But not both cheeks.

Joshua Banks was the only one.

He tipped his skateboard, jolting to an abrupt stop seconds before smashing into her. It would have been a pleasant smash, Rilla thought.

"Hi, Earth," Joshua said. "Has anyone saved you yet?"

True, it was a corny joke, but she always laughed. It would have been rude not to.

"Hi." Rilla hoped he couldn't tell by looking at her that she'd just read forty-five valentines in his honor, and none was good enough for him.

He raised his shoulders, hiking up his jacket, shoving his fingertips into his jean pockets. He looked so-o-o-o cute when he did that.

"Do you get to come with us on Friday?"

Rilla assumed "us" meant the other home-schoolers. "Where?"

"To see the traveling exhibit at the History Museum."

She shrugged. Had Sparrow forgotten to tell her? "What's it about?"

"The Tower of London."

"Oh." *How could there be an entire exhibit on one tower?*

Joshua stamped a foot onto the skateboard to keep it from rolling away. "It's this tower where a bunch of people got their heads chopped off, and . . ." He paused, squinting at the overcast sky as if the "heads chopped off" part was all he remembered after hearing a much longer explanation. "Well, anyway, it sounded cool."

"Oh." *Say something besides "Oh."* "I don't know. My mom hasn't said anything about it yet." She tried not to chomp her gum in front of him. He'd think she was a baby, still chewing bubble gum.

"My mom's supposed to call your mom today."

"Oh." *Brilliant, Rilla.*

Joshua spun his skateboard around and shoved off. "Hope you can come!" he called back over his shoulder.

Rilla watched him fly down the street until he turned a corner and disappeared from sight. *Hope you can come! Hope you can come!* singsonged over and over in her head, warming her so much she feared the heat might melt the frozen yogurt in her backpack.

Pedaling home, Rilla grumbled to herself. Why hadn't she said something intelligent? Like *Oh yes, the Tower of London. Why, I read a book on it when I was only five.*

Of course, it would have been a fib.

Regardless, she hoped Sparrow agreed to the field trip. Learning about a place where people got their heads chopped off would certainly liven up an otherwise boring Friday.

Then the rest of Joshua's words sunk in. The exhibit was at the History Museum—a two-hour drive from Harmony House, meaning the field trip would last all day.

Rilla'd never left the monsters alone without popping in to check on them every hour or two. She'd never been gone an entire day.

Icicle would probably be fine. But what about Sweetie Pie?

And what about leaving the two alone together for that long?

Was spending the day with Joshua Banks worth any disaster that might happen in the attic while she was at the museum?

Rilla weighed the pros and cons as she steered her bike down Hollyhock Road. With mental apologies to the monsters, she realized her choice was obvious.

She *must* spend the day with her one true love.

11

The Fight Scene

Rilla's alarm beeped, waking her from a familiar dream about her father. He'd come knocking on the door at Harmony House, bearing twelve birthday gifts for Rilla—one for each year he'd missed—plus presents for every Christmas past.

Funny, he didn't look at all like his picture. He looked exactly like Mr. Tamerow, right down to his Australian accent.

The recurring dream usually ended with a giggling Sparrow coming to ask Rilla to be maid of honor at their second wedding.

That's how Rilla *knew* it was a dream. Sparrow never mentioned *him,* other than voicing her standard excuse for the split: "*Being young was our mistake,*" she'd say, as though *young* was something a wise person would never be.

This time the dream ended with her father rescuing his beloved daughter from an attic full of vicious monsters. (Okay, so bubble-gum-and-Popsicle-eating monsters weren't exactly vicious; it was only a dream.)

Shaking the fantasy from her mind, Rilla climbed out of bed. Halfway to the bathroom, she stopped. A basket of magazines lay overturned by the door. Tufts of fur—silver and pink—littered both sides of the room.

What happened last night? Rilla put one hand to her head, trying to remember.

Sparrow had gone out to attend a meeting on the future of the city's garbage. Rilla and Aunt Poppy had stayed up late, crying through an old movie called *Love's Last Look*. (According to her aunt, the dashing hero resembled her first husband, which is why *she* was sniffling. Rilla sniffled every time *any*one in *any* movie left *any*body who loved them.)

After the movie, Rilla had slipped into the attic without turning on a light. She hadn't wanted to rouse Sweetie Pie because the monster made her read the same bedtime stories over and over. (*Her* favorite book was *Pinkerton*.)

Rilla remembered going into the bathroom. The bath mat was squishy wet, and the tub hadn't been drained. Those two things should've immediately tipped her off that something was wrong. (Icicle was good about cleaning up after himself, although sometimes he forgot to flush.)

So, what had happened in her absence?

Rilla checked on the sleeping monsters. Icicle lay curled in a fluffy ball on what used to be her favorite pillow. He looked almost angelic. (Key word: almost.)

Sweetie Pie snored away, half buried under a stuffed pink flamingo borrowed permanently from Rilla's bed.

One thing confused her. A shirt from her closet had been ripped in two. Each monster had obviously claimed half for its fortress.

Ever since Sweetie Pie arrived, she'd been slowly decorating her home with Rilla's pink clothes. But why would Icicle fight her for one shirt?

Rilla peered at Icicle's half—now serving as a pillowcase. Dotted randomly across the material were tiny pink Popsicles.

Aha! No wonder. The monsters' idiosyncrasies had overlapped.

Tiptoeing around the attic, Rilla cleaned up the mess, grumbling to herself about the room being "big enough for one and all" until she realized she sounded like Sparrow spouting her aphorisms.

After a quick shower, Rilla rubbed herself dry, trying to rub away her worries as well. Why did the home-schooler field trip have to be today? No way could she stay home and monster-sit. And she couldn't separate Icicle and Sweetie Pie; the bathroom door didn't lock.

To keep from waking them, she dressed quietly,

set out plenty of monster food, then penned a note to the literate monsters:

Dear Icicle and Sweetie Pie,

I won't be in to check on you until late afternoon. (Sorry, S.P.) Please nap or play nicely while I'm gone. Be *good*. Be *quiet*. And *behave*.

Yours,
Rilla

She hoped it worked.

12

Ghosts and Guillotines

Outside, Rilla waited on the veranda with Sparrow for the other home-schoolers to arrive.

Finally the minibus they'd rented for the day came barreling down Hollyhock Road with Mrs. Welter at the wheel. Tina's mom was the oldest—at least fifty-something. She'd taught school for years, so when she finally married and had a daughter, she chose to combine teaching with motherhood by home-schooling Tina.

In her teal leather jacket with a glittery design, Mrs. Welter looked like Tina, minus the spiked hair. *Her* hair sported a killer perm—stiff ringlets held in place with industrial-strength mousse.

The minibus crunched gravel as it turned into the driveway. Rilla and Sparrow were the last to be picked up, so they had to sit in front behind the driver.

Rilla wasn't pleased about spending the two-hour drive sitting next to Sparrow, surrounded by everyone else's mothers, while the other six home-schoolers sat in back, laughing and talking.

It was so humiliating.

Especially since Sparrow had insisted on wearing her whale sweater. On the front, a humpback carried a picket sign in his flippers. It read: SAVE ME.

Rilla thought it was funny, but she'd rather Sparrow blend in with the other denim-and-craftsy-shirted mothers. The other kids already thought the Earth family was weird. Why give them more ammunition?

The rearview mirror provided Rilla with a good view of everyone. First there was Wally Pennington (a.k.a. Wally Penguin). A bit chubby, he swayed side to side when he walked, and his nose was more like a beak.

But he was smart—and he'd actually visited the *real* Tower of London.

Next to Wally sat Andrew Hogan. Andrew had moved here from Australia, so his accent sounded like Mr. T.'s. (Right now he was loudly complaining about the cold weather, and how seasons are reversed in Australia.) Cold Julys and hot Januarys sounded strange to Rilla.

Behind Wally and Andrew sat Marcia Ruiz and Kelly Tonario. They'd been in Rilla's class at Pickering and she liked both of them.

Marcia, quiet and serious, was taller than everyone, even the mothers. Her dark French braid hung to the back of her thighs. Kelly was the opposite of Marcia: clipped blond hair, short and stocky, a goofy sense of humor.

Behind them, guess who? Joshua and Tina. Laughing at Andrew's complaints. Rilla tried to convince herself they'd been forced to sit together, but she knew Tina had probably arranged it. . . .

• • •

Inside the History Museum the air was freezing. Everyone left coats and sweaters on.

Rilla was glad she'd worn her padded jean jacket with a picture of the world embroidered on the back. The word EARTH curved across the top in fancy letters. She thought the double meaning was clever, proud she'd designed it herself.

The group split up, wandering through the museum in twos and threes. The exhibits were nifty—definitely worth the drive.

First thing Rilla discovered was that the Tower of London wasn't a tower at all. It was a fortress. So, why didn't they call it the *Fortress* of London?

She didn't ask, afraid Tina might whisper, "Dumb, dumb, dumb," like she did sometimes when Rilla asked a question.

"Why is it called a *tower* when it's really a *fortress?*"

Rilla's question came from Kelly as they strolled

past exhibits of knights' chambers and fifteenth-century coats of armor.

"Good question," Mrs. Welter said.

Rilla kicked herself for letting Tina's intimidation keep her quiet.

"The tower was built first," Mrs. Welter explained. "Then the fortress around it, but the original name stuck." She zipped her glittery jacket against the brisk air. "Anyone know what happened inside the tower?"

"Yeah," Joshua blurted. "People got their heads chopped off."

"Ewww," Tina groaned, coyly smacking his arm.

Rilla turned her back so she didn't have to watch Tina's sickening attempts at flirting.

"Wait a minute." Wally's penguin nose disappeared inside a brochure. "Prisoners were *tortured* in the tower, but lost their heads outside on the Tower Green."

"Yeah, so they could wash away the blood," Andrew added, reading over Wally's shoulder.

"Ewww," the seven of them groaned in unison.

"The Tower Green is where Queen Anne Boleyn lost her head on the chopping block," Andrew read. "And her ghost has been seen wandering under the window of the room where she spent her final days."

Rilla grimaced at Andrew's lighthearted reading of gloom and doom. She stepped past pictures of dungeons and torture devices, looking for something more pleasant to study.

Like Joshua Banks, who was peering at the ax and guillotine chopping-block display.

Tina grabbed his arm and yanked him down another aisle.

Rilla followed.

"Hi, Earth," Joshua said with the same dimply grin he'd given the guillotine.

Tina yawned, as though Rilla's presence bored her.

"Look at the ravens," Joshua said, pointing at the stuffed black birds hunched on a turret.

Rilla complied, stepping closer to the display.

"If ravens ever desert the tower," Joshua read. "It's believed that the fortress will fall, and so will the kingdom."

"So the ravens' wings are clipped to make them

stay," Tina finished. She glanced at Rilla. "Hey, what are *you* looking at?"

"The ravens," Rilla answered, bristling. Joshua had pointed them out to *her,* not to Tina. "I know a *lot* about ravens," she added, then bit her lip. What compelled her to say *that*?

"You know a *lot* about ravens?" Tina smirked, giving Joshua a nudge.

He didn't respond, which pleased Rilla.

"So *tell* me about ravens." Tina stepped in front of the display, blocking Rilla's view. "What do ravens eat?"

Without thinking, Rilla snapped, "Cowpeas."

Surprise reddened Tina's face while Joshua laughed. "Good answer, Earth," he said.

Rilla whipped around and headed toward another display.

Score one for me, she thought, wondering if black-eyed peas actually counted as raven food. . . .

• • •

On the ride home, Marcia fell asleep, so Rilla and Kelly sat together, trading jokes along the way. The ones Rilla thought funniest happened to be monster jokes:

Why did the monster hug his girlfriend to death?

He had a crush on her.

Where do monsters go on vacation?

To Lake Eerie.

How does every monster book begin?

With a dead-ication.

After the monster jokes, Rilla had a hard time concentrating on other puns and riddles—or on Tina's further attempts at flirting with Joshua Banks.

She kept picturing her attic bedroom as a mini Tower of London. The monsters weren't exactly prisoners, but they were locked inside, weren't they? No, she wasn't torturing them—but what if they were torturing each other? Her thoughts drifted to the tufts of monster fur she'd found scattered across the floor this morning.

Sighing, she slumped in her seat and closed her eyes, pretending to sleep so she could panic in private.

The ride home was the longest two hours of her life.

13

Monster on the Loose

As the minibus returned to Harmony House, darkness settled over the neighborhood like an inky omen.

Rilla's gaze flew to the attic windows as soon as the bus rounded the last curve on Hollyhock Road.

The lights were on. Good sign? Or bad?

Were the monsters reading? Napping? Killing each other?

While Sparrow said thank yous and good-byes to the others, Rilla bolted from the bus and raced toward the veranda.

"Hey!" Sparrow called. "You forgot to thank Mrs. Welter."

Rilla stopped under the B & B sign and aimed a cheerful wave at the bus. She *liked* Mrs. Welter; it was her grumpy-as-Icicle daughter she could do without.

Inside, Rilla dashed up the stairs, counting them as she climbed (a habit she'd picked up when she was younger). Including the veranda steps, there were forty-seven in all from ground to attic. No wonder she was always out of breath by the time she got there.

Heart pounding, Rilla unlocked the attic door, letting it swing open before stepping inside. Twangy music met her ears. A voice wailed about "Papa dyin' in his boots."

Rilla tiptoed inside and caught her breath.

Icicle's fortress was in shambles—the chair upended, shoe boxes smashed. Tiny goose feathers from his pillow frosted the area as if a hailstorm had pelted the fort. The monster's books (*her* books) lay scattered open-faced across the floor like fallen birds.

Rilla twirled to assess damage in the rest of the attic. Everything else looked normal. The tornado had touched down only in Icicle's corner.

"Icicle?" Rilla called softly. "Sweetie Pie?"

A humming sound led her to the closet. Inside sat Sweetie Pie, quietly coloring on the wall with a pink crayon.

"Don't!" Rilla snatched the crayon from her paw, wondering how she'd ever clean greasy pink scribbles off the wall.

Sweetie Pie began to sniffle.

"Where's Icicle?" Rilla demanded, as if expecting a verbal answer.

Acting as grumpy as a two-year-old who's missed her nap, Sweetie Pie grabbed for the crayon, but Rilla shoved it deep into her jean pocket. Sweetie Pie was *not* going to be any help.

Quickly Rilla toured the rest of the attic. Icicle wasn't in his usual spots. The tub was dry, which immediately rang alarm bells in her head. Icicle never missed his daily bath.

Rilla yanked Sweetie Pie from the closet. "Where *is* he?"

The monster set a firm paw on each chubby hip and jibber-jabbered what sounded like a plea of self-defense.

A sick feeling punched Rilla in the stomach. How could Icicle be gone? The door was locked from the outside and the windows didn't open. There was no way out except . . .

Rilla felt the blood drain from her face. She dashed into the bathroom. The lower cabinet door was ajar. And the only thing *inside* the cabinet was the laundry chute.

Sweetie Pie peeked around the bathroom door.

"You didn't!" Rilla hissed.

If monsters could grin—that's what the pink monster did.

Rilla tore down the back stairs to the kitchen (thirty-seven steps). Aunt Poppy was setting bowls on the table while Sparrow dipped homemade vegetable soup from a clay pot.

"Just in time," Sparrow said, placing a steaming bowl at Rilla's place.

The homey smell of simmered-all-day soup made Rilla's mouth water. But how could she eat with a monstrous knot in her stomach? First she had to find Icicle and smuggle him back to the attic before anyone saw him.

What if he ran into B & B guests and gave them heart attacks? *She'd* be responsible.

"How was your field trip?" Aunt Poppy asked. Tonight she wore a jean skirt and silky blouse, her hair loose and curled—a refreshing change from her cleaning-clothes attire. (José must be back, Rilla thought.)

"The field trip was fine." Her answer was abrupt; she wasn't in the mood for small talk—not with a monster on the loose.

Sparrow handed her a tin of soda crackers. "You'll

have to say more than 'fine' when you write your field trip wrap-up for class," she teased.

Rilla set the cracker tin on the table, then nonchalantly worked her way toward the basement stairs.

"It's time to eat," Aunt Poppy said. "Where are you going?"

"I— I need fresh towels."

"Now?" Sparrow asked. "Can't it wait till after dinner?"

"Um, I'm letting my soup cool." Rilla slipped backward through the basement door before Sparrow could stop her.

"Need any help?" her aunt called.

"No!" All Rilla needed now was for Aunt Poppy to stumble over a midget monster napping among the folded laundry.

"By the way," Aunt Poppy hollered down the stairs. "You've been using towels like they wash and fold themselves. Can you cool it, please?"

Rilla chuckled. Should she tell her that a bath-loving monster demanded a fresh towel every day? Or that the monster who preferred long showers refused any towel that wasn't pink? Ha!

Seventeen steps to the basement. Rilla raced to the basket where clothes from the laundry chute dropped. A deep indentation dimpled the middle of the damp towels, as if something heavy had landed.

Something like a monster.

So it was true. Icicle lurked somewhere in the basement, like the pesky spiders who zoomed out of nowhere and scared her.

She let go of the breath she was holding, relieved that the towels had broken Icicle's four-story fall.

Rilla tried not to picture what she *might* have found if the laundry basket hadn't been there. Why did the words from the song "Monster Mash" suddenly pop into her mind? Yuck.

"Icicle!" Rilla whisper-yelled. "Where are you?"

Flipping on extra lights, she inspected each corner. The basement overflowed with years of accumulated *stuff*. Antique furniture waiting to be refinished for the B & B rooms was stacked in one corner. Christmas decorations filled another. Boxes and boxes and *boxes* of belongings from all her aunt's marriages blocked Rilla's way.

"Your soup's getting cold!" Sparrow called.

"Coming!"

There were a million places Icicle could be hiding. Yet something poked at the back of Rilla's mind. Would the monster hide from *her*? She was his source of food and comfort.

What if he refused to return to the attic? Was he still in love with the she-monster who'd dumped him down the laundry chute?

Rilla couldn't help but laugh. She'd give a year's allowance to watch a videotape of the fight scene that had raged in the attic while she was gone.

Stepping past a closet filled with out-of-season

clothes, her laugh caught in her throat. Boxes here had been rearranged; she could tell by the dust on the floor. They'd been scooted and stacked to reach a high window.

The window was open. No way would a basement window be open in February.

Icicle had escaped to the outside world!

Alone.

And dangerous?

No. But different. An oddity. If someone called the dog pound to report a strange animal, surely they'd pick Icicle up without a fight. *He'd* think they were coming to wait on him, paw and claw.

Rilla shivered in the damp basement. What would they do to him? Donate his body to science? Dissect him to see what he was?

Icicle wasn't easy to love. Still, he *belonged* to her now. She was responsible for him, and she wished him no harm.

In fact, she couldn't quite explain the tightness choking her chest. In spite of Icicle's orneriness, Rilla was scared for him.

He needed her.

She perched on a wooden crate to sort out mixed emotions. Maybe when Mr. Tamerow got here, he'd know how to handle the monsters.

What if he makes you tell Sparrow? And what if she makes you ship them back to their homelands?

"No!" The word sounded loud in the quiet basement.

Why not? They've brought you nothing but frustration.

True. But sending them back seems cruel. I'd be rejecting them; returning them to the orphanage—or the monster factory.

Why did thoughts of her father pop into her mind again? Sadness tinged the edges of her heart. How could he reject his own daughter? Didn't he care whether or not *she* needed *him?*

Well, *she'd* never reject anyone who needed *her.* No way would she ever return her monsters.

"What are you doing down there?" Sparrow shouted. "Weaving the towels from cotton yarn?"

"Coming!"

Rilla left the window open. If Icicle got scared out there in the vast, unpredictable world, at least he'd have a way to get safely inside.

Grabbing a pile of clean towels (to support her excuse), she hurried up the steps to dinner.

Now all she needed was *another* excuse—a reasonable one—for going outdoors on a dark winter's night.

14

Going on a Monster Hunt

"Didn't you feed the kittens this morning?" Sparrow asked, clearing the table after dinner.

"Yeah." Rilla shook her prop—a bag of Friskies. Hidden inside were a flashlight, a pillowcase, and a hair band. "Now that the kittens are bigger, they eat more." (It was true.)

Rilla went out the back door. Pulling her flashlight from the bag, she clicked it on, looping the beam in quick circles around the patio. Had she really expected to find Icicle sitting in a lawn chair like the lady from Utah?

Ha—too easy.

Now what? Would Icicle be hanging out in the yard? In the neighborhood? Or was he hitchhiking to the nearest coast to catch an ocean freighter across the Atlantic for home?

She laughed at the image of the little monster thumbing rides with his paw, panhandling change for

Popsicles and frozen yogurt. Maybe he'd wear a disguise, like a baseball cap and sunglasses, although Rilla thought seven-eyed sunglasses might be hard to find.

She circled the house calling, "Here, Icicle; here, boy," making it sound as though she were calling a dog in case anyone might be listening.

No luck.

Well, if he wasn't in the yard, he was probably gone for good—unless he showed up tonight on the eleven o'clock news. The thought made Rilla's skin prickle with dread.

Discouraged, she danced the flashlight beam along a pathway of round flagstones as she made her way to the barn. Hugs from a warm kitten or two seemed the only thing that might comfort her right now.

Rilla entered the barn and waited, inhaling the scent of damp wood mixed with cat. Usually the kittens heard her coming and bounded from their napping spots to greet her, yet none came. Where were they?

"Oreo?" Rilla called. "Milk Dud? Here, kitties."

When they didn't appear, she assumed they were nursing. Hoisting the Friskies bag under one arm, she climbed the short ladder to the loft to check Oreo's favorite spot.

A lumpy pile of fur confirmed her theory. The kits had nursed, then fallen asleep cuddled together to ward off the nippy air.

Rilla aimed the flashlight, smiling at the confused, blinking eyes that greeted her.

Wait a minute. There were too many eyes.

"Icicle!" Rilla dropped to her knees for a closer look. One of the lumpy bumps in the furry pile was a monster. His silver fur wasn't cat colored, making him an obvious intruder.

Icicle's head lay on Oreo's rump; Dorito and Pepsi cuddled close, one under each hairy arm, and Milk Dud sprawled across the monster's legs.

Laughing at the strange sight, Rilla felt so relieved, she wanted to cover Icicle with kisses—if he'd let her.

The cats accepted the monster as one of their own. She wondered if they understood monster talk, or if Icicle could translate mews and purrs.

As soon as the kittens sniffed Friskies, they peeled themselves from the pile. Rilla scattered a handful of crunchies on the floor to keep them busy while she confronted Icicle. He'd raised to his elbows, glowering at her as if to say: *It's about time you found me. Where's my dinner?*

She pulled the pillowcase from the bag. Should she throw it over him and dash to the attic before he realized what was happening? Or should she logically explain the situation? She chose the latter.

"You have to go back to the attic," Rilla told him.

Icicle cocked his head. His hair was sleep-ruffled, as if it needed a good combing. And the question in his eyes was obvious.

"Yes, Sweetie Pie is still there. But I promise *never* again to leave you alone with her for a whole day." (She wasn't sure how she'd uphold this promise, but she'd think of something.)

No reaction from the monster.

"Your food is in the attic—unless you prefer cat crunchies."

That did it. Icicle stood, brushing off cat hairs. Then he padded toward the ladder.

"Hold it." Rilla grasped his scrawny shoulder. "You can't parade through the B & B like you belong there. What if you ran into someone? You have to go back in this." She opened the pillowcase.

With an insulted look he returned to his warm spot with Oreo.

"If you stay here, you give up bath time."

He didn't move.

"No more books. No pillows. No Walkman. No rocking chair."

Icicle gave a whiny groan. Coming up on his back paws, he stood tall. With a haughty look he stepped willingly into the pillowcase.

Rilla closed the top with the hair band, then heaved the heavy pillowcase over one shoulder and carried it down the ladder. She stopped to fill cat dishes with crunchies, until grumblings from the pillowcase made her hurry on.

Leaving the Friskies bag behind, Rilla stumbled

across the yard in the dark, stealing around the house to the veranda. Chances of running into Sparrow or Aunt Poppy were slimmer if she avoided the living area in back.

Crouching low, Rilla peered through a window. The lady from Utah was on her way to the parlor where guests were provided with espresso coffee and herbal teas twenty-four hours a day, plus television, newspapers, and magazines.

At the front desk a new guest was registering. *Great timing, Rill.*

Both Aunt Poppy and Sparrow were there—her aunt checking the guest in, and Mom handing him a mug of something.

Was it Mr. Tamerow? For an instant Rilla's heart surged with hope. Then the man turned sideways, and his bearded silhouette gave her the answer.

Why hadn't Mr. T.'s letter told when to expect him? He always liked to surprise them by showing up unexpectedly. Once when the B & B was full, Sparrow had to set up a futon in the classroom for Mr. T. to sleep on.

Rilla sighed. "Oh, Mr. Tamerow, *please* come before monster number three arrives," she whispered into the darkness.

The thought of a *third* monster in the attic made her cringe. What bad habits would the next one burst upon the scene with?

Rilla stayed crouched by the window until Aunt Poppy led the new guest upstairs to his room. Sparrow followed, carrying his bags.

Single suites were on the blue floor, so Rilla knew she'd be safe if she took the front stairs to the green floor, then the back stairs to the attic, skipping the blue floor altogether.

Quietly she slipped through the double doors, hoping not to attract attention from guests in the parlor. Clutching Icicle in her arms like a baby, she took the steps two at a time. Grunts and groans coming from the pillowcase told her Icicle was *not* enjoying his bumpy ride.

As she neared the end of the green hall, a family from Florida tumbled out of G-8, blocking her way. Rilla put her head down, kept a tight grasp on the pillowcase, and implored Icicle to shut up for at least ten seconds.

"Whatcha got there?" the father asked, waving an unlit pipe. (Sparrow made guests go outside to smoke.)

Rilla tried to hurry past the family, but they didn't move.

"Let *me* see!" cried a toddler dressed from head to toe in red dinosaur-print pajamas. Rilla couldn't tell if it was a boy or girl.

"Uh, it's—" She gave Icicle an abrupt squeeze, hoping he'd quit squirming.

"Doggie?" the kid asked.

"No, um—"

"Kitty?" Dinosaur arms reached for the pillowcase.

Rilla flattened her back against the wall and scooted past them. "I can't—"

"Show me!" the kid screamed.

"No!" Rilla screamed back.

The parents aimed disapproving frowns at Rilla. "Our child loves animals," the mother said, patting "it" on the head, "so if you could just give us a quick peek, we'd—"

"This . . ." Rilla paused, praying the family wouldn't tell Sparrow her daughter had yelled at them. "This is a project for school." It wasn't a lie. She'd searched every book she could find on southern Africa, trying to spot any mention of Botswana-bred monsters. "It's a *secret* project," she added for the benefit of the kid of undetermined gender.

"Oh, well then." The mother seemed to probe for a shred of logic in Rilla's explanation. "Come, love." She took the dinosaur kid's hand.

Rilla dashed toward the back stairs. Tearful whinings of "I wa-a-a-nna se-e-e-e i-i-i-i-i-t," echoed in her ears.

"That was close," she whispered to Icicle as she reached the attic. "Thanks for not cooperating."

Rilla stepped inside and slammed the door, pausing for a long sigh of relief. She dumped Icicle onto the floor, letting him fight his own way out of the pillowcase. Wadding it up, he stuffed it under one arm and took it with him, as if to prevent Rilla from ever forcing him into it again.

Stalking to his corner, he calmly began to rebuild his fortress, ignoring Sweetie Pie, who stood in her little house, nibbling a pink carnation while playing dress-up in Rilla's pink baggy sweater and—

Rilla gasped.

On top of Sweetie Pie's head perched a floppy, pink-ribboned hat sporting a side cluster of pink sand plums.

15

Crime and Punishment

"How did you—?"

Rilla stopped. She knew how. In her haste to find Icicle, she hadn't locked the door. Sweetie Pie must have sneaked from the attic, then ransacked somebody's room.

The lady from Utah's room.

"You stole that hat!" Rilla's voice flew up two octaves. "And that ring!"

Sweetie Pie grasped the pink garnet band hanging from her ribbon necklace, trying to hide it.

"What else?" Rilla shrieked. "Where did—?"

She was so flustered, the words wouldn't sputter out. What if Sweetie Pie stole from *other* rooms too? What were the chances of more than one guest forgetting to lock the door?

"Give me the hat." Rilla dove into Sweetie Pie's fortress.

The monster scrambled over the desk and waddled

toward the door. Rilla crossed the room in two steps and locked it.

Now the only exit from the attic was the laundry chute—which Sweetie Pie knew well.

Rilla grabbed her desk chair, hurried it into the bathroom, and shoved it against the cabinet.

Sweetie Pie retreated into the closet, slamming the door.

Rilla slumped to the floor outside the closet, counting to ten to calm herself. Would reason work with Sweetie Pie? It worked with Icicle.

She glanced at him. He'd stopped rebuilding his home to watch the chase scene. White goose feathers were stuck to his silver fur. The expression on his face was as close as it could get to *See? She's not as sweet as we both first thought.*

"Sweetie Pie," Rilla began, her voice exuding more patience than she felt. What she felt was the urge to wring one little pink neck.

The closet door clicked open.

"I've given you a home," Rilla told her. "I give you fresh flowers to eat every day; all the bubble gum and fruit punch you want. I let you raid my closet, take my pink clothes, use my radio, my shower, my jewelry."

She paused, squinting into the closet to make sure someone was listening.

Behind a tennis racket, two narrowed eyes reflected the light.

"Anything your little pink heart desires, I give you, Sweetie Pie. There's no reason for you to steal. Stealing isn't *nice*."

Now she sounded like Sparrow again.

A pink paw thrust the hat through the crack in the door. The sand plums were missing.

Rilla cleared her throat. "In New Zealand, do they put monsters into jail for stealing?"

The plums came flying out. Next came the ring, a pink button, a coral brooch, and a pink envelope addressed to a Mrs. Kunichev of Provo, Utah.

"Oh, no," Rilla groaned. The robbery was more extensive than she'd suspected.

Gathering the stolen property, Rilla peeked out the attic door. The coast was clear. Maybe the lady—Mrs. Kunichev—was still in the parlor.

Could Rilla smuggle the items back to her room before she returned? Or before she called the police?

Rilla's heart nearly stopped at the thought of police swarming the B & B, searching for the robber. Eventually they'd make it to the attic. Then she'd be arrested.

For what? Harboring mischievous monsters?

Rilla tiptoed down the attic stairs. What room was the lady from Utah in? She had to be on the blue floor, in one of the single suites.

Rilla hesitated. No way could she go down to the front desk and look in the register for the lady's room number without attracting attention.

Aunt Poppy always stayed in the area to take care of travelers arriving after dark. Early mornings and evenings were the busiest times for guests checking in and out.

What should she do? Try every door on the blue floor until she found one unlocked? For lack of a better plan—yes.

B-6. Quietly she turned the knob. Locked.

B-5. Turn the knob. Locked.

Rilla felt like a criminal. Breaking in to *leave* valuables instead of *take* them. Sparrow would murder her if she knew.

B-4. The knob turned. Rilla's heart skittered. As she opened the door, it sprang from her hand. The new guest with the beard gaped at her. "May I help you?" he asked.

"I— I was looking for . . . Oh! This is B-4," Rilla gushed. "My mistake."

He glanced at the items she carried. "Are you selling things door to door?"

"No, sir. Sorry to bother you." Rilla backed down the hallway, trying to grin. *Trying* because her lips were shaking from fear.

The man gave her an uncertain smile and shut the door.

B-3. Rilla turned the knob. The door opened. She waited for the occupant to confront her.

No one was there.

She tiptoed in. A lady's dress lay on the bed. Aha. The suite belonged to a woman. The one from Utah?

A pink letter lay on the writing desk. The gold heading matched the return address on the pink envelope.

She was in the right room. Now. Where should she put the stolen property?

Quickly Rilla dumped everything on the bed, and reattached the sand plums to the hat. She slung it over the antique hat tree, then placed the ring, button, and brooch on top of the dresser, and the envelope on the desk.

"What are you doing in my room?"

Rilla's heart jumped out the top of her head.

Mrs. Kunichev towered in the doorway, like the evil villain in a horror movie, blocking the heroine's only escape route. (Only Mrs. Kunichev wasn't evil and Rilla wasn't a heroine.)

"I . . . the . . . my . . ." A million excuses jumbled through Rilla's mind.

"I the my?" the lady repeated, fingering the beads around her neck as though she thought she'd better hold on to them or Rilla might snatch them and run.

Maybe truth was her best defense. "You see," Rilla began. "My, um, *pet* got loose and found its way into your room."

"Your pet?"

Rilla nodded. "You forgot to lock your door," she added before the lady could ask what *kind* of pet.

"It—my pet—ran off with a few of your belongings, and I was simply returning them." She held up empty hands to prove she wasn't stealing anything.

"Hmmm," the lady hmmmed.

"Mrs. Kunichev, please don't tell my mother. It's my fault that my pet got out of its, um, cage. It won't happen again." Rilla tried to look sorry, because she was. Sorry she'd gotten caught when Sweetie Pie was the scoundrel.

"Well, as long as you came into my suite to *return* things." Mrs. Kunichev's gaze skipped around the room as if taking inventory. "I'll forget it happened."

"Oh, thank you, thank you." Rilla could have hugged her. She circled the lady and backed into the hallway. "Remember now, keep your door locked."

"I will." The lady studied Rilla's face as though she might have to identify her later in a police lineup. "Good night," she said, closing the door.

Rilla heard a click as the lock slid into place. She collapsed against the wall, waiting for her heartbeat to return to normal.

"I wonder," she whispered to herself, "would they put *me* into jail for *murdering* a monster?"

16

Prisoners in the Tower

Rilla patted the sticky salt-and-flour paste one last time, smoothing the Kalahari Desert on her relief map of Botswana.

One of the baobab trees was cockeyed, so she straightened it. The "tree" was actually a fat twig off the hackberry out by the barn, but on her map it represented a baobab.

She stepped back to survey her work, wiping gooey hands on a towel.

To her, the country's outline resembled the head of a lizard. Its eye was Lake Xau (made with one of Aunt Poppy's zodiac collector thimbles—Taurus—sunk deep in the paste and filled with water).

The lizard's tongue, flicking out from a pointy nose and mouth clear on into the next country, was the Limpopo River (made with a meandering blue ribbon).

Rilla wondered if this river was the same "great grey-green, greasy Limpopo River, all set about with fever-trees," where Rudyard Kipling's Elephant's Child with his " 'satiable curtiosity" got his nose stretched into a trunk by the Crocodile. If so, it would be one more fact to add to her Botswana report for Sparrow.

Sighing, Rilla glanced around her room, making sure all was well. She'd spent the entire weekend locked in the attic, standing guard over the monsters. Prisoners in the Tower of Harmony.

She'd left the room only to do chores, eat, and feed the kittens. Hints of spring were in the air—two robins in the larch pine, buds on the pussy willows, and a faint shimmer of green across the lawn. Yet here she was indoors, monster-sitting. Boring, boring, boring.

Actually, Rilla didn't mind staying out of Aunt Poppy's way. After forgetting to remove Sweetie Pie's pink crayon from her jeans pocket, it'd tumbled through the laundry, melting in the dryer, ruining a load of clothes, including her best jeans and Aunt Poppy's favorite cleaning T-shirt. (It read: MULTICULTURAL PLANET SEEKS HARMONIOUS RELATIONSHIP WITH ECOLOGICALLY MINDED SPECIES. SEND PHOTO.)

Aunt Poppy hadn't quite gotten over it yet.

Oh well. Staying in the attic meant she'd finally caught up with her homework.

Rilla placed the relief map by a sunny window to dry, then washed her hands and started the next project—gluing white lace onto the red-paper valentine she was making for Joshua Banks. (She'd bought *pink* paper, but Sweetie Pie snitched it off her desk and wallpapered her fortress with it.)

After the glue dried, Rilla scouted for a large envelope so she wouldn't have to fold the valentine. With her best pen she printed Joshua's name, using her left hand so he wouldn't recognize her handwriting.

Later she'd take it to the community mailbox and slip it through the Bankses' slot so Joshua would get it tomorrow.

Now for the special message. What should it say? Standard valentine stuff? Naw. Too corny, too sentimental.

She wanted something special, yet secret. From her to him.

From Rilla Harmony Earth to Joshua ? Banks.

She wondered what his middle name was. Probably

something strong and noble. Like Abraham, Mr. Tamerow's first name.

Joshua Abraham Banks. J.A.B. She loved it when someone's initials spelled a word. She wished hers did too; then she and Joshua could have secret names for each other, and no one (meaning Tina Welter) would know what they were saying:

"*Good morning, Jab.*"

"*Hello, Rhe.*"

See? It didn't work. But if she *married* him someday, her initial name would be *Rheb.* Now, *that* worked. . . .

Back to the valentine. And a proper sentiment.

What was the nicest thing one person could say to another?

Let there be rain popped into her head.

Well, yeah, if she were in Botswana. But Joshua would read it, then shake his head and say, "Huh?"

Rilla wandered the room, thinking. Icicle slouched in the rocker, reading *Some of My Best Friends Are Monsters.*

Across the room, Sweetie Pie hummed the pickup-truck song as she flipped through an old copy of *Sassy.*

"I've got it!" Rilla rushed back to her desk. With her right hand (so it would look neater) she wrote:

> To Joshua Banks,
> Let there be love.
> From ?

It was perfect.

17

Worms in the Rain Forest

By Monday morning Rilla was more than ready to leave the attic. To her relief, calm had reigned the entire weekend. The monsters read, played (by themselves), or napped. She felt confident they'd leave each other alone for a few hours.

Making sure the door was locked, she carried the relief map downstairs to turn it in, along with her final report.

Then she circled the classroom, watering plants. Not just any plants, of course. Sparrow's collection of plants that removed toxins from the air.

The philodendron and peace lily absorbed polluted air and released pure oxygen all day. At night, they stopped photosynthesizing while two other plants, a bromeliad and an orchid, took over.

Last, Rilla watered the ivy—a plant she'd talked Sparrow into buying simply because she wanted a *normal* plant in her classroom. A plant without a job to do.

Today was Valentine's Day. And one of two days each year the home-schoolers' Charity Project Committee met. The committee included all of them, since the project was actually a social-studies assignment.

Rilla was excited about the home-schoolers' meeting at her house this time, although she hoped Sparrow and Aunt Poppy didn't do anything to embarrass her. (Last time, Aunt Poppy met everyone at the door in her BRAN KEEPS YOU GOING! T-shirt, then called them *children*. Rilla could've died right there on the veranda.)

She set a store-bought valentine by each place at the round table. On the front of the valentines, a kitten who looked just like Milk Dud said, "Get your paws on a terrific Valentine's Day." She'd signed Joshua's card "Earth," since that's what her one true love called her. She hoped he noticed.

"I'm finished with the oven!" Sparrow called.

Rilla hurried into the kitchen to prepare a pan of Botswana brownies.

Last time the home-schoolers met, Sparrow had fixed basmati rice cakes topped with tofu blended in soy milk and sprinkled with chopped kiwi and pepitas. Nobody even touched them. Nobody'd even *touched* them.

The only way Rilla had convinced Sparrow to let her serve a treat as sinful as brownies was to convince her:

1. The home-schoolers would actually eat them.

2. The brownies were part of her hands-on assignment on Botswana.

3. She promised to make them from whole-wheat flour, carob, honey, and organic walnuts.

While the brownies cooked, Rilla ate breakfast. Then she mixed nonfat milk and Sucanat (unrefined sugar retaining all the vitamins, minerals, and trace elements of a natural sugarcane plant). Setting a small bowl of the white mixture aside, she added mashed blueberry juice to the rest.

Rilla smoothed the blue icing onto both sides of the brownies, leaving a wide space in the middle. There she laid a thick stripe of black licorice (from a health-food store) end to end, then finished with a stripe of white icing on each side of the licorice.

Standing back, she compared the iced brownies to a picture of the Botswana flag. Perfect. A thick black stripe bordered by two thin white stripes was set on a light blue background.

"Very nice," Sparrow said over her shoulder. "Extra credit we can eat."

Soon the other home-schoolers arrived, gathering around the table to munch brownies. Mothers didn't join the group, but stayed in the room to listen to the discussion—and referee when needed.

Andrew Hogan, chairperson of the Charity Project,

called the meeting to order. "We've received eight requests for donations since our last charity meeting. How much money do we have?"

Marcia Ruiz answered, since she was the treasurer: "We *should* have $182.00—a one-dollar-a-week donation from each of us since last August. But we only have $176.00."

"Six dollars short?" Wally Pennington blurted. He could figure math in his head faster than Rilla could say "penguin."

The group peered at each other, as if ferreting out the guilty one.

Rilla squirmed in her chair. Ever since the monsters moved in, she hadn't had spare dollars to donate. "We're, um, each allowed to withhold our donation during emergencies," she explained in a wavery voice. "Remember? It's one of our rules."

All eyes landed on her like vultures.

Sparrow, eyebrows raised under her long bangs, silently mouthed the word "Emergencies?" to Rilla. Other mothers looked relieved it wasn't *their* offspring withholding money from the homeless and hungry.

"So, what'd you do with our money?" Tina Welter demanded. She seemed pleased Rilla was the guilty one.

Rilla didn't like the way she called it *our* money.

"She doesn't have to explain," Joshua Banks said. "That's a rule too."

Rilla could've hugged him. (Well, she could've

hugged him for *any* reason.) Still, it was nice of Joshua to stick up for her. She nodded at Andrew to go on with the meeting so everyone would quit gaping at her.

"Okay," Andrew said. "Do we want to divvy up the money and send an equal amount to each charity?"

"No." Kelly Tonario whipped open her notebook and grabbed a pen. "Some charities may deserve more than others, and some we may not want to support at all."

"And some," Wally added, "can be our priority next time we meet, which allows us to send more to those who need our support right now."

The debate was on. An hour later Andrew read the final choices.

Two charities would receive donations next time they met.

One they trashed. (A celebrity was collecting money to save worms in the rain forests. They decided other needs were more urgent.)

Of the remaining five charities, fifty dollars went to:

- a fund for feeding homeless children

- a boy at Pickering Elementary who'd had an emergency kidney transplant

Twenty-five dollars went to:

- a nearby animal shelter that needed to expand

- a natural-disaster fund to help earthquake, flood, and tornado victims

- a fund to preserve South American rain forests (the whole forest, not just the worms)

"We have one dollar left," Marcia said. "I move we put it back into the box for next time."

"All in favor?" Andrew asked.

Seven hands shot up.

Rilla's guilt over the missing dollars gave her an idea. "Hey," she said, getting everyone's attention. "Instead of stuffing our dollars into an old shoe box, why don't we open a charity account at the bank so our money can *earn* money?"

After a moment of quiet contemplation, Joshua exclaimed, "Cool idea, Earth."

"Yeah," everyone but Tina echoed. They voted in favor of Rilla's idea even before a motion was made. (Tina voted too, after Joshua held up her limp arm.)

Sparrow winked at her daughter as she bit into a Botswana brownie.

Rilla gave a relieved sigh.

She'd been redeemed.

• • •

After school Rilla dashed to the attic, pleased to be greeted by monsters snoring in nonharmonic rhythm instead of by the aftermath of a hurricane.

She sprawled on the bed, eager to open her valentines. All but two were standard sentiments. Tina's card featured an ugly gorilla on the front. Rilla took it as a personal insult—especially since Tina had put a hyphen between the *o* and the *r*, making it "go-rilla." The card read: *From one swinger to another, Happy Valentine's Day.*

Joshua Banks's card was a drawing of planet earth. Rilla's skin prickled in goose bumps. He'd picked it out special, just for her.

An earth card.

It read: *Peace on Valentine's Day. Pass it on.*

Rilla grinned at the words, feeling a whole lot better about her bird-mother and flower-aunt.

Joshua Banks understood her weird, weird family.

18

What Lurks Inside a Mailbox

In Rilla's dream, she was dashing down Hollyhock Road, rushing the newest monster box from the community mail to the attic.

Once there, the box exploded in a spray of colorful fireworks.

Stepping from the smoke was a red, white, and blue monster.

The July Selection.

He scattered confetti knee-deep in the attic, woke guests with noisemakers, and consumed vast amounts of hot dogs, apple pie, and root beer.

Rilla fidgeted in her sleep.

Snow fogged the next dream as a candy-cane-striped monster wearing a Santa cap and eating fruitcake played endless Christmas carols on her tape player.

The December Selection.

Rilla moaned.

Then a dark, robed figure moved toward her in a threatening way. The creature peeked from under his black slouch hat and grinned. Sharp pointy fangs much longer than Icicle's were stained red with blood.

Her hand flew to her neck. Had the vampire monster bitten her? Or attacked the other monsters? The October Selection was evil. He plotted to overthrow Harmony House for his own wicked purposes.

Rilla jolted awake. Sitting up, she grabbed a pillow to protect herself from the dream monsters. Was this a nightmare? Or real?

Sounds of contentedly snoring monsters filled the attic. "There are only two here, Rilla," she said out loud. "Calm down."

Yeah, but today is the start of a new month.

"Ohmigosh."

The first day of March.

Rilla fell back and closed her eyes, feeling doomed. What waited outside in the mailbox? Maybe if she left it there, it would go away.

It won't go away, Rilla.

"What if I wrote 'Return to sender' on the box?"

The monster might starve to death on the trip home.

Rilla knew she could never allow that to happen.

Icicle snorted.

Rilla clicked on a lamp to see what he wanted. Seven eyes blinked irritably in the light. He hated it when she woke him.

Hopping from the rocking chair, he glared at her over the edge of his fortress. His eyes seemed to say, *Who the heck are you talking to?*

"I'm having a conversation with myself," she told him. "You got a problem with that?"

With a final snort he climbed back into the rocker and pulled a pillow over his head.

The alarm was about to beep, so Rilla got out of bed.

In spite of the foreboding dream and her fear of this morning's trek to the mailbox, an exciting fact prevented her from going back to sleep.

Today was her birthday.

Rilla stumbled into the bathroom and gazed in the mirror. "March first!" she exclaimed. "My thirteenth birthday!"

She brushed her hair, then straightened, trying to

look taller, older, more mature—now that she was a teenager.

Didn't work.

She peered sideways at her profile, hoping to see some hint of a future figure.

Disappointed, Rilla groaned at her reflection. "Columbus was wrong after all. Earth is definitely flat. . . ."

She laughed at her own dumb joke. "N.F., Rilla. Not funny."

Showering and dressing, she moved through her morning rituals like a zombie. Forget her birthday. All she could think about was the monster lurking in the mailbox.

Would the March Selection be friend or foe? Would he (or she) get along with the others? This one could be worse.

"It's March!" Rilla called to Icicle and a sleepy-eyed Sweetie Pie, wanting to prepare them. Did they understand? Did they sense another of their own was near? Would they make room for one more in the attic?

The monsters stared at her the same way Tina Welter did whenever she accused Rilla of being weird.

Trudging downstairs as though she were off to face one of Sparrow's oral exams on a topic she'd never heard of, Rilla greeted a few early risers.

Grabbing the mail bag, she headed out the door, following the sidewalk to the privacy-pine gate.

"Good day, mate!" hollered a familiar voice.

Rilla stopped. A taxi was pulling into the driveway. Leaning precariously out the back window was Mr. Tamerow, wildly waving at her.

"Mr. T.!" Rilla yelped, dashing across the yard. "You're here!"

Mr. Tamerow stepped from the taxi and gave her a fatherly hug. "I wouldn't miss your birthday now, would I?"

He was tall and thin, constantly in motion. Excitement hovered around him like honeybees over a rosebush. And the top of his head was bald, as though he moved so fast, his hair couldn't keep up, and it dropped right out of the race.

Mr. Tamerow wore his balloon-leg pants from India and his rainbow-striped coat from Guatemala. On his head was a Siberian herdsman's hat with his luggage keys pinned to the side so he wouldn't lose them.

Flourishing one arm, he bowed, handing her a gift. "Happy birthday!"

While he paid the cabbie, she dropped to the ground and opened the package, knowing Sparrow would rather she waited till "time to open gifts." Digging through tissue paper, Rilla pulled out a white stuffed polar bear.

"It's from a town in Alaska called Shaktoolik," he told her.

"Shaktoolik," she repeated, liking the sound of the

word. She hugged the newest addition to her stuffed-animal collection, then bounced to her feet to hug Mr. Tamerow again.

Rilla was so glad to see him, she skipped sideways all the way to the veranda, babbling about how much she missed him and all the things she wanted to tell him—meaning monster news.

But not now. There were too many people around. She'd have to talk to him alone, prepare him for the shock, then take him to the attic.

He piled his bags inside the door and waved at Aunt Poppy. Rilla set the polar bear and wrappings on the sideboard, then went back outside.

"Where are you off to so early?" he asked.

"To get the mail."

"Fine, I'll go with you." Mr. Tamerow started down the veranda steps.

Rilla froze. Yes, she wanted to tell him about the monsters, but not like this. Not by taking him to the mailbox and giving him cardiac arrest when he saw the March monster's package wiggling and jiggling in the box.

"Aren't you going to register first?" she asked.

"Well, I waved at Poppy. That's as good as registering when you've been here as many times as I have."

"Oh," Rilla answered. *Now what?* She backed up the veranda steps. "It's time for breakfast; I'll get the mail later."

"Aw, come *on*, Rilly." Mr. Tamerow grabbed her hand and pulled her along. "I've lots to tell you, and it's a school day, so we'll chat till it's time for your lessons."

Snatching the mail bag from her hand, he yanked open the gate, enthusiastically leading the way to the mailbox—and whatever monstrous *thing* was lurking inside.

19

Mystery of the Monster Club

"Did you get my postcard from Alaska?" Mr. Tamerow asked as they hurried down Hollyhock Road.

"Yes. How was your trip?"

"Fabulous." His eyes sparkled as they widened and narrowed with his words. "I must have heard your favorite song a million times while I was there."

"The pickup-truck song?"

"Yes. Alaskans love country music."

They arrived at the mailbox.

Rilla stalled.

Should she peek inside and tell him it was empty? The mail hadn't arrived yet? Her birthday was a national holiday, so there'd be no mail delivery today?

Maybe he won't notice a bulging box splattered with foreign stamps.

Right, Rilla.

"So, have you been getting any . . . uh . . . *interest-*

ing mail lately?" His eyebrows went up and down a few times; then he held her gaze as if he was *dying* to tell her something.

Rilla caught her breath. "You!" she yelped. "It was *you!*"

He feigned surprise. "Me? What did *I* do?"

A wave of weakness washed over Rilla until her knees gave out. She plopped onto the curb to think. Of *course*. It was Mr. T. who'd signed her up for the Monster of the Month Club. How could she ever have suspected anyone else?

She almost felt like crying. A small part of her *still* wanted to believe her father had something to do with the gifts.

Give it up, Rilla. You've never even met him. Why would he suddenly start sending you presents?

"Because he's my *father*," she mumbled. "*That's* why."

"What's that?" Mr. T.'s long legs folded as he sat beside her on the curb. "Are you okay, Rilly?" He cocked his head, concern flickering in his eyes. "Oh, my, do I see tears?"

Rilla whisked the tears away and jumped to her feet. *What's wrong with you? Mr. T. is here. He's confessed. You've solved the mystery of the monster club—so why are you crying?*

"I'm sorry." Rilla sniffled a bit and rubbed her cheek to erase any sign of tears. "I'm okay. I just . . .

well, I *suspected* you were the one who sent the gift—
but I wasn't sure. Until now."

"Don't you *like* them?" he whispered, as if worried
about upsetting her again. "I thought it'd be the perfect gift for you. A whole year's worth of stuffed animals for your collection. And they're all *monsters*—
which I thought was a clever idea."

He came to his feet. "Did I make a mistake?"

Rilla shook her head, but her mind never got past
his words: *stuffed animals.* He thinks they're *stuffed*!
He thinks they're *toys*!

"I love the monsters; really I do." Smiling, she
squeezed his hand to reassure him so he'd stop gaping
at her like he'd committed some terrible social error.

"You really do like them," he stated.

"Yes!"

Mr. Tamerow glanced at his watch. "Well, today's a
new month. Let's see if the March Selection has
arrived." His dark eyes sparked in anticipation.

Tell him.

How? I can't just blurt it out. He won't believe me.

Then show him.

Rilla opened the mailbox. She snatched letters and
mailers, stuffing them into the bag Mr. T. held wide.

The box was there. It was hard to ignore.

Why couldn't she leave it behind and come back for
it later?

Alone.

"There it is!" Mr. Tamerow grasped the box and yanked it out of the mailbox before Rilla could react.

He peered at the label with great curiosity. "Mmm. This one's from Limerick, Ireland." He laughed as though it was funny. "You don't suppose he spouts poetry, do you?"

"They don't talk."

Rilla cringed. The words had jumped out of her mouth before she could stop them.

Mr. Tamerow gave her a goofy look. "Well, of *course* they don't talk. I was making a joke." He nudged her with his elbow. "You were supposed to laugh."

She gave a weak chuckle.

"Let's go back to the house and open the package. I want to see if you're getting my money's worth."

Rilla's chuckle caught in her throat. "You mean, you want to o-o-open it?"

"Yeah, I want to o-o-open it. But not here. Let's get inside where it's warm. I'm sure Poppy will have a thermos of hot chocolate in the parlor."

He shoved the box into the mail bag, which made Rilla breathe a sigh of relief. That way he wouldn't notice if the package started wiggling.

She had to walk fast to keep up with his long strides.

Think, Rilla, her mind implored. *What are you going to do now?*

Plans and excuses bumped recklessly into each other as she tried to sort them out. Maybe she could get the box away from him, and—

Tell him! The sooner, the better. Tell him NOW!

At the edge of the privacy pines, Rilla put on the brakes.

"What is it, mate? Something *is* bothering you; I can tell." Mr. Tamerow knelt on the sidewalk so they were eye to eye.

Rilla took a deep breath. Avoiding the truth any longer was pointless. "I've something to tell you," she began. "About the monsters."

"Yes?" He grinned a bit too eagerly.

She tried to grin back, but those darn tears were only a blink or two away. Whenever Mr. T. arrived, it always made her think about her father—which was dumb. Mr. Tamerow didn't have anything to do with her father. But if she ever got a chance to order one from a dad catalog, he'd be just like—

"Well?" Mr. T. interrupted her thoughts. "You said you *liked* the gift. Does it upset you that they're monsters, and not regular animals?"

"Oh, no. That's not it." Rilla knew she was unintentionally hurting his feelings, and it made her feel horrible. "It's just . . . well, what would you think if I told you the monsters were . . . um . . . real?"

There, she'd said it.

"Real?" he repeated. "You mean *real* as in *alive*?"

She nodded, holding her breath, watching his eyes.

Mr. Tamerow threw back his head and gave a great hooting laugh, making the keys on his herdsman's hat jingle.

Rilla stared at him. She didn't know what reaction she expected, but it certainly wasn't hilarity.

Coming to his feet, he pulled his wallet from a pocket inside the Guatemalan jacket. "You're talking about the legend, right? Isn't it fabulous? I saved a copy for myself." He took out a folded paper and handed it to her. "I often collect legends from the countries I visit."

Legend? Rilla squinted at the words, then read out loud:

"Legend of the Global Monsters

"Once, when stranger things than monsters roamed the earth, these tiny creatures shared nature with us, living in small colonies scattered throughout the world. Belief held that spotting a mini-monster in the wild meant good fortune would follow for a year.

"Today, likenesses of the monsters have been created as cozy collectibles. Yet, legend warns, when stars line up in angled shapes like lightning, real monsters tread the earth once more."

"Isn't it wonderful?" Mr. T. gushed, returning the paper to his wallet.

Rilla was speechless. *Weren't legends just—legends? Or was it possible for some to be true?*

"Come on," he said, opening the gate. "Let's go meet your newest cozy collectible."

Rilla, in a daze, followed him across the front yard.

Her worst nightmare was coming true.

20

The Moment of Truth

"Welcome to Harmony House, Abe," Sparrow called to Mr. Tamerow as she set a bowl of pomegranates on the dining-room table. "I put your bags in suite B-1." Reaching into her apron pocket, she pulled out a key and tossed it to him.

"Thanks, mate," he said, making a perfect catch. "Always glad to be here." He handed the mail bag to Rilla, then shrugged out of his coat. Underneath, he wore a Hawaiian shirt splashed with pink orchids. (Rilla hoped Sweetie Pie didn't rip it off him when he stepped into the attic.)

Dumping the mail onto the sideboard, she clutched the box against her side, trying to make it look inconspicuous.

Guests filed into the dining room from the parlor and down the stairs. Mrs. Kunichev entered. She peered suspiciously at Rilla over the top of her glasses, then sidestepped around her.

"Hey," called a familiar voice from the landing.

José *was* back. Rilla waved at him, angling her body so he couldn't see the box as he came down the stairs.

She waited while everyone took seats around the table. What was she waiting for? The box was in her hand. All she had to do was bolt up the stairs. Then her monster secret would stay a secret.

"Come." Mr. Tamerow gestured toward the table. "Open your birthday gift and show everybody what you got."

"Here?" Panic shot up inside her like a Roman candle.

Murmurs of "Happy birthday" echoed around the table. A few guests toasted her with glasses José was filling with grapefruit juice.

"Th-thank you," Rilla stammered.

She could *not* open the box here. What would happen when the monster jumped out? Rilla pictured guests diving under the table, racing for their rooms, screaming, and fainting.

Then, journalists with cameras and microphones would swarm the veranda, filming her as police led her away for terrorizing B & B guests with a secret weapon.

She shook her head to dissolve the images. Business at Harmony House would be ruined. All because of Rilla and her monsters.

"She's too shy to open her gift in front of us," the

bearded man from B-4 offered, commenting on her hesitation. Rilla figured he wanted her to leave so he could dig into Sparrow's six-grain pancakes.

Mr. Tamerow stepped across the room to coax Rilla to the table.

Sparrow appeared, intercepting him. "Come into the kitchen and join us for breakfast while Rill opens her presents," she whispered. "You're like one of the family anyway."

Rilla used to wish Mr. Tamerow would marry one of the Earth sisters so he *could* be one of the family. But Sparrow and Aunt Poppy always fussed over him as though he was the brother they never had.

Maybe it was better if he *didn't* marry into the family. They'd insist on changing his name to something weird—like *Boulder* or *Tree*.

Perhaps it was better for him to remain, in her mind, as a model for the perfect Earth Father.

Meanwhile, Mr. T. was thanking Sparrow for her offer to join them.

"I'm honored," he said, facing the other guests. "You're right. The birthday girl is too bashful to open her gift here. Besides, she has a pile of others in the kitchen."

The guests laughed and waved them away.

Rilla followed him into the kitchen. She should've felt relieved at not having to open the box in front of the B & B guests.

Only she didn't. Now, instead of scaring off strangers (except José), she'd scare off her own family.

A pile of gifts (wrapped in recycled paper) filled the middle of the kitchen table. Rilla set the monster box on the floor under her chair and took her place. Aunt Poppy served Belgian waffles (Rilla's favorite), fresh melon, and hot ginseng tea with a dash of peppermint.

Sparrow handed her the gifts one by one. Rilla *oh*ed and *ah*ed in all the right places as she unwrapped them.

She got a charm bracelet of endangered species. New underwear (what an embarrassing gift to open in front of Mr. Tamerow). Two tickets to one of José's concerts. A sweater from Aunt Poppy that read: HAVE YOU HUGGED YOUR EARTH TODAY? (Rilla wondered if Joshua Banks would get the hint when she wore it.) The last present was a mug that said: UNI-VERSE MEANS ONE SONG FOR ONE PEOPLE.

Rilla slipped the bracelet onto her wrist, then dug into her waffle.

Mr. Tamerow took hold of her other wrist. "If you don't open your last birthday present right now, *I'm* going to." He rescued it from the floor and playfully bonked her on the head with it. "You've kept me in suspenders long enough."

They laughed at his dumb joke.

With shaking hands, Rilla tore off the packing tape as slowly as she could, then ripped the end of the box.

Aiming the opened end away from everyone, she tensed, waiting for a monster to come barreling out—and be as crotchety as Icicle or as fussy as Sweetie Pie.

Rilla closed her eyes. *This is it. My secret's out.*

Nothing happened.

Aunt Poppy snickered. "You think it's going to walk out of the box on its own?"

Yeah, Rilla said to herself. Out loud, she answered, "No, ma'am."

Carefully she peeked inside. Reaching in, she pulled out . . .

A stuffed animal.

A stuffed monster, to be exact.

Its fur was green. A tiny bowler hat perched on top of its head, held in place by stiff round ears like mouse ears. Under its collar was a green bow tie.

"How cute!" Aunt Poppy squealed, snatching it from Rilla's grasp.

Rilla stared as Aunt Poppy cuddled the green monster.

It's not alive.

The shock made her dizzy.

It's stuffed. A stuffed toy.

She held on to the edge of the table to keep from falling out of her chair.

"Earth to Earth," Sparrow said. "Mr. Tamerow asked if there was anything else in the box."

"Oh." Rilla shook it. A piece of paper fell into her lap. She read out loud:

Monster of the Month Club

March Selection
Name: Shamrock   *Gender:* Male
Homeland: Ireland
Likes: Clover, raw potatoes, and green ginger beer
This one is a party monster.

"Shamrock," Rilla repeated, rereading the "birth announcement."

Green ginger beer? Did Mr. Baca's One-Stop Shoppette carry *that*? And clover was seasonal. Feeding this one would've been tough.

The words that bothered Rilla most were "party monster." Wouldn't *that* add lots of excitement to her attic situation—ha!

"What do we say to Mr. Tamerow?" Sparrow's singsong tone was the same one she'd used on Rilla at age four.

"Oh—thank you," Rilla said. "For giving me Shamrock. And the others."

"Others?" Aunt Poppy echoed. "What others?"

"Well, you see," Mr. Tamerow began, answering for Rilla. "Shamrock is one of a dozen selections in the Monster of the Month Club."

"Monster of the Month Club!" Aunt Poppy squealed again, jabbing Rilla's arm with Shamrock's head. "You mean you've gotten other monsters?"

Rilla nodded. *Oh boy, here it comes.*

"Why didn't you tell us?" Sparrow asked.

"Well, they're just . . . toys," she finished, her voice a bit weak.

"Just toys?" Sparrow mimicked. "Oh, I get it. Ms. Rilla Harmony Earth is thirteen now. Maybe she's too *old* for toys."

Mr. Tamerow stuck out his bottom lip, giving her a hurt-puppy look. It made him look ridiculous, especially since he still wore his herdsman's hat with the floppy ears on each side.

"No, I *love* stuffed animals," she told them. "I'll never get rid of my collection—no matter how old I am."

Rilla grasped Mr. Tamerow's hand. "Honest."

He pursed his lips as if he didn't quite believe her.

Aunt Poppy was still enthralled with Shamrock. "Abe, however did you learn about the Monster of the Month Club?"

"Last fall I had business in Oklahoma, and I met the president of Global Gifts Incorporated." He paused, helping himself to another cup of tea. "His company was preparing to launch the monster club, with the first gift shipping out of Gaborone."

"Gaborone," Sparrow repeated. "Why does that name sound familiar?"

"It's a lovely city in—"

"Botswana," Sparrow finished for him. She turned to her daughter. "Aha. Pieces of this puzzle are beginning to snap into place."

"I want to see the other monsters," Aunt Poppy insisted, sounding like the whiny red-dinosaur kid.

Rilla felt blood drain from her face. Her arms. Her body. She was dead. No doubt about it.

"How many have you gotten so far?" her aunt asked.

"There should be two," Mr. Tamerow said. "The January and February selections."

Everyone was staring at her. She had to say *something.* "You're all coming to my attic?" Her voice chirped like a baby bird's.

"Heavens, no," Aunt Poppy said. "I climb stairs all day. I'd never go all the way to the top floor unless I absolutely had to."

Whew, Rilla moaned to herself. *Close call.*

"*You* run up and get them," Aunt Poppy ordered. "And bring them down to us."

Rilla's rump was cemented to her chair.

"Dear, are you all right?" Sparrow felt the side of Rilla's face to see if her daughter was feverish. "You act as though you're on another planet."

"I'm fine." Rilla wished she *was* on another planet. Or in Ireland or New Zealand or Botswana. *Anywhere* but here.

"Well, then, *move*. Poppy asked you to run upstairs and get the other gifts Abe sent you."

Rilla rose from the table, slow as a minute. She took Shamrock from Aunt Poppy's outstretched arms and carried him toward the back stairs.

Was it possible to disappear between the first floor and attic and never be seen again?

Highly improbable, her mind pointed out.

Rilla headed up the stairs, willing the improbable to happen.

21

How to Impersonate a Monster

One, two, three.

Rilla counted steps as she climbed.

She stopped on the first landing to study Shamrock. He was the same size and shape as the other monsters. But he wasn't alive. Why not? Had he been left in the box too long?

Ten, eleven, twelve.

Think, Rilla. What are you going to do?

You CANNOT take Icicle and Sweetie Pie downstairs.

First of all, Icicle won't let you touch him, and second . . .

Rilla pictured the flabbergasted looks on everyone's faces when she bounded into the kitchen with two live monsters.

Monsters with attitudes.

Eighteen, nineteen, twenty.

Wait a minute.

The grown-ups didn't know what Icicle and Sweetie Pie looked like. They expected stuffed animals.

That's it! All she had to do was return with two of her stuffed animals. No one would know the difference.

Rilla climbed faster in excitement.

Brown Bear could be Icicle. For Christmas, she'd gotten earrings shaped like tiny icicles. She could poke them through the bear's ears.

And the pig! Good ol' Penelope Pig could be Sweetie Pie. She was a lovely shade of pink. Rilla could stick her red heart pin into Penelope's fur to make her look Valentiney.

What a brilliant idea! (She'd also have to rescue poor Penelope from the pink fortress. The pig was being held captive by a monster with keen fashion sense.)

Twenty-eight, twenty-nine, thirty.

"Now, don't tell," Rilla whispered to Shamrock, then bounded up the rest of the stairs.

Thirty-six, thirty-seven.

Rilla unlocked the door and rushed inside. She snatched Brown Bear off the bed, replacing him with Shamrock, who fit right in with the others—although he was the only green one.

Grabbing her earrings, she stuck them through Bear's ears, wincing although she knew he couldn't feel it. After all, he was only a stuffed toy.

"Icicle, look," Rilla said, carrying the bear to the

monster's corner. "Brown Bear's going to impersonate you, and—"

Rilla froze.

Icicle hunched in the rocker, as usual, a book in his lap.

Only it wasn't Icicle. It was a stuffed monster, made of cotton or wool or whatever stuffed toys are made of.

Rilla dropped the bear and reached for Icicle, holding him at arm's length for a good look. It was him all right—bushy silver tail, seven eyes, pointy fangs. Only he didn't move. Didn't look at her. Didn't bat her hand away or grumble-growl.

"Icicle!" Rilla's voice was high-pitched and squeaky. "What happened to you?" She hugged him to her chest. "Sweetie Pie, look!"

Rilla raced across the attic. Sweetie Pie leaned against the towel cabinet, half in, half out of Rilla's pink halter top. She was playing dress-up. The tape player hummed the way it did whenever a cassette reached the end and nobody was there to flip it over.

Rilla scooped the pink monster into the other arm. "Sweetie Pie!" She slumped to the floor beside the fortress, feeling as though someone had punched the wind out of her.

Staring from one to the other, Rilla began to cry. They looked so . . . so much like themselves. Only they weren't there anymore. No spark in their eyes. No fire.

Why are you crying? she asked herself.

They were a pain. A bother. Now they're gone.

"Gone," she repeated. "No. They're still here with me."

Get serious, Rilla. You should be happy. You couldn't have kept the monsters here forever. You couldn't keep adding a new one every month.

I know.

It wasn't logical. Someone would've found out.

Right. And they'd have been taken away. To a zoo. Treated like animals.

"And you're *not* animals, are you?" Tears rolled down her cheeks. "I'd never let them treat you like animals. Ha—*you'd* never let them treat you like animals."

Rilla stared into Icicle's eyes. All seven of them. Searching for some flicker of . . . of what? Recognition? Grumpiness? Need?

She hugged them both. "It was nice to be needed."

Suddenly she was sobbing. Partly for the monsters. Partly for the ache of people coming and going in her life. Icicle and Sweetie Pie had arrived, needing her. Now they didn't need her anymore.

B & B guests came and went. Many she got to know, but she tried not to get too attached. They always left.

Now the tears were for her father. He didn't need her or he'd come back and never leave again.

Next the tears were for Mr. T. She was already too attached to him. She loved him like a father, yet he was gone more than he was here.

And lately she'd been getting too attached to funny José, who always found time to talk. Had he come back to see her? Or Aunt Poppy?

Clank, clank, clank.

Sparrow's banging on the pipes meant, *Did you forget to come back?*

Pulling herself to her feet, she gently set the monsters on the bed, wiped her eyes, and straightened her clothes.

How could she face the grown-ups and act normal? Wouldn't they notice she'd been crying? Over a couple of silly stuffed toys?

Scooping Sweetie Pie and Icicle into her arms, Rilla held her head high, then carried them down to the kitchen for monster show-and-tell.

22

What Strange Magic?

Rilla finished her bedtime rituals, then wandered around the attic, feeling lonely. She'd never forget her thirteenth birthday.

Scooting Icicle's rocker (*her* rocker) back to where it used to be, she stacked shoe boxes in the closet and returned books to their shelves.

Moving to Sweetie Pie's corner, she carried the wicker cabinet and shower rug to the bathroom. Rounding up all the pink clothes the monster had borrowed (stolen?), she dumped them down the laundry chute.

Rilla chuckled when she pictured Aunt Poppy washing clothes this week, wondering why all of Rilla's laundry was pink.

Sighing, she left the rest of the rearranging for tomorrow.

Usually before bed, Rilla moved her stuffed animals to a chair, then chose one or two to sleep with. Tonight the choice was easy. She pulled back the covers and leaned Icicle and Sweetie Pie side by side against the pillow, paws touching.

Icicle must be in monster heaven, she thought. He was touching Sweetie Pie—and she couldn't retaliate.

Rilla watched them, waiting for a brief movement or whimper.

"He called me from a truck stop in Albuquerque," she sang, hoping for a glint of recognition in Sweetie Pie's eyes. Or for her to grab the cowboy hat off the bedpost and pull Rilla along with a step-step-kick. *"Oh-h-h-h, oh, Oklahoma . . ."*

Rilla's voice trailed off. Sweetie Pie didn't react any more than Shamrock did.

Well, no use sitting here watching them all night. Waiting for them to chitter and cluck at her when it wasn't going to happen.

Rilla reached for the polar bear, whom she'd officially named Abraham after Mr. Tamerow. Giving him a good hug, she set him on the windowsill and picked up Shamrock.

Then, for the zillionth time, she went over the whole scenario in her mind. Mr. Tamerow had ordered stuffed toys. When they arrived, they had been alive. Until today.

What strange magic caused the change? Mr. T.'s arrival? Her birthday? Or had stars *really* lined up in angles shaped like lightning?

Had the turn of the earth broken the pattern? Ending the magic? Ending the monsters' life cycle?

Tomorrow she'd go to the library and find Ms. Noir. Once, when Rilla was studying constellations for school, the librarian had showed her a whole section of books on astronomy. *She'd* know what books to look in.

Rilla hoped Ms. Noir could *also* answer a question that'd been poking at the back of her mind ever since Mr. Tamerow had shown her the legend: When the proper angle of stars occurred over various parts of the earth, did the magic happen in different countries at different times?

Meaning, could these monsters—or those to come— spring to life once more? The thought both intrigued and frightened her.

Rilla hugged Shamrock. "Welcome to the family, you party monster." Down deep, she wondered if she'd ever see this one alive.

Maybe she should make up her own monster legend: *When the full moon falls on the tenth day of a month having eight letters—monsters will walk the B & B once more.* Ha!

Don't laugh, Rilla. It could happen.

Maybe someday she'd get a job like Mr. Tamerow's. Travel the globe. Visit Botswana, New Zealand, Ireland. And ask for a tour of their cozy-collectibles factories.

A noise drew Rilla's attention to the attic door. A letter had been slipped underneath. Setting Shamrock on the windowsill, she sprang off the bed to get the letter.

A note in Sparrow's handwriting was attached to the envelope: *This was mixed in with my mail.*

It was from Joshua Banks! A birthday card!

Rilla sat on the floor and ripped open the envelope. The card was handmade from white construction paper. On the front he'd drawn two arms holding hands. Inside was a penciled message:

To Earth,

Let there be Friends.

From ?

Her heart leaped to the ceiling and back. He'd signed it with a question mark, yet he'd called her Earth. No one else called her that.

Wait. The sentiment was almost identical to her mushy valentine. He knew she'd sent it! And he wanted her to know this card was from him.

Now Rilla knew what to do with that second concert ticket from José.

Was this the luck the legend promised would come if you spotted a live monster? If so, her thirteenth year promised to be a good one.

Rilla dug in the bottom dresser drawer for the cookie tin. A card from Joshua Banks (her one true love) was worthy of her treasure collection.

Sprawling on the quilt, she started to open the tin, but something caught her eye.

Icicle was right where she'd left him. But Sweetie Pie was not. She teetered on the edge of the bed, as far from Icicle as she could get.

Rilla stared at them, waiting for fur to start flying. She *swore* the monsters' paws had been touching when she left the bed.

Was she imagining things?

Rilla put Joshua's letter in the cookie tin, keeping one eye on Sweetie Pie. Climbing under the covers, she

clicked off the light and snuggled close to her monsters of the month, one on each side. Together, yet apart.

Then Rilla closed her eyes to sleep.

She could hardly wait until April.

I'll Love You Till My Pickup's Lost its Shine

Copied by Rilla Harmony Earth
Guitar chords figured out by Aunt Poppy (with José's help)

He called me from a truck stop in Albuquerque.
(G)
I screened it on my answerin' machine.
(G) *(D)*
When I heard his voice, Lord I started cryin'.
(G)
Thought I'd never hear from that cheatin' man again.
(G) *(C)* *(G)*

Chorus:

Oh-h-h-h, oh, Ok-la-ho-ma.
(D) *(G)*
You locked me up and throw'd away the key.
(D) *(G)*
Oh-h-h-h, oh, Ok-la-ho-ma.
(D) *(G)*
That wanderin' man'll be the end of me.
(A) *(D)*

"I'll love you till the redbuds stop their bloomin'."
A lie like that could melt this heart of mine.
But the words that made me his alone forever:
"I'll love you till my pickup's lost its shine."

(Chorus)

That night he sent a bouquet made of rose rocks.
It should have been a warnin' when it came.
Where he's concerned, my heart is soft as petals,
but his stone heart will never ever change.

(Chorus)

He told me he was flyin' in to see me.
Then asked me if I'd hold there on the line.
While he grabbed up his guitar and played so tender:
"I'll love you till my pickup's lost its shine."

(Chorus)

J
Regan, Dian Curtis.
Monster of the Month Club

	DATE DUE	